## "You sure you want to play this game?"

Maggie laughed at Cale's words. She knew without a doubt she was playing with fire, but the slow burn of desire in the pit of her tummy was too intoxicating for her to walk away now.

The wicked grin on his face should've scared her off, but instead of hightailing it to safety, she deliberately crossed the kitchen toward him. "When I play," she told him, "I play to win."

His laughter warmed her as he set the dishes on the counter. He turned and slowly peeled the filthy T-shirt over his head, revealing inch by delicious inch of his well-tanned, muscular torso.

She itched to smooth her hands over the texture of his skin, to press her lips to that glorious wall of flesh. As she wrestled with the wisdom of her actions, he tossed the shirt aside and reached for her. With his hands locked firmly on the swell of her hips, he backed her up against the refrigerator and pressed his body into hers.

"So do I," he whispered, his breath hot against her ear. "And I won't lose."

Dear Reader,

The idea for SOME LIKE IT HOT first came to me when one of my closest friends decided to pursue a new career, that of an EMT followed shortly thereafter by her successfully becoming a firefighter. Our discussions during her education and training fueled my creative fire to the point I could no longer ignore the three sexy hunks you're about to meet.

This month, meet Cale, a hot and sexy paramedic with a penchant for saving damsels in distress, something that often leads him into trouble. Every man loves a mysterious woman, but what could be more intriguing than a woman without a past...especially a past she can't remember?

Join me again in October, when a blistering *Heatwave* isn't all that's heating up for arson inspector Drew. Will this diehard playboy finally torch his little black book? In November, things get even hotter when firefighter Ben comes *Under Fire* when he's asked to fulfill the ultimate fantasy—of the woman investigating him.

I would love to hear from you! Feel free to drop me a line anytime at P.O. Box 224, Mohall, ND 58761 or jamie@jamiedenton.net. Be sure to stop by my Web site at www.jamiedenton.net for the latest hot and steamy news!

Until next month,

Jamie Denton

# Books by Jamie Denton

**HARLEQUIN TEMPTATION**
708—FLIRTING WITH DANGER
748—THE SEDUCTION OF SYDNEY
767—VALENTINE FANTASY
793—RULES OF ENGAGEMENT
797—BREAKING THE RULES
857—UNDER THE COVERS

**HARLEQUIN BLAZE**
10—SLEEPING WITH
    THE ENEMY
41—SEDUCED BY
    THE ENEMY

# Jamie Denton
# SLOW BURN

HARLEQUIN®

TORONTO • NEW YORK • LONDON
AMSTERDAM • PARIS • SYDNEY • HAMBURG
STOCKHOLM • ATHENS • TOKYO • MILAN • MADRID
PRAGUE • WARSAW • BUDAPEST • AUCKLAND

For Crystal Denton

Acknowledgments:
My first trilogy for Harlequin Temptation would never have become a reality
if it wasn't for the help of a few people. First, Leslie Nielsen. Without her patience
in answering my questions these stories would never have been possible.
To the crew of the Somers Fire Department, for generously sharing their time
and expertise. My editor, Jennifer Green, for always making me look good.
My agent, Ethan Ellenberg, for his wonderful guidance and support.
And, as ever, Tony, my own special hero,
for his love and steadfast encouragement.
I wouldn't be here without any of you.

ISBN 0-373-69142-4

SLOW BURN

Visit us at www.eHarlequin.com

**Printed in U.S.A.**

# 1

"WHAT'S YOUR NAME, sweetheart?"

She looked up into the clearest, bluest eyes this side of the Rockies and would've sighed with pleasure if her throat didn't feel so darned ragged. All she could do was blink before her world tilted again, and those sexier-than-sin eyes swam before her blurred vision. Her head ached, her chest burned and a searing pain gripped her right arm. Someone said it was because of smoke inhalation, but she couldn't be sure.

She tried to shake her head to clear the haze, but a pair of large, warm hands held her still. Her head rested against a pair of rock-hard thighs she assumed belonged to the black-haired angel of mercy who'd hefted her over his shoulder and carried her from the burning building seconds before the explosion.

What she was doing in a paint warehouse, she couldn't say.

"You got a name, honey?" he asked again in a rich, soothing voice that made her think of silly things like white picket fences, children's laughter and golden retriever puppies.

"Maggie." She tried to shake her head again, but he held her still. *Maggie?* That wasn't right. Or was it? "I think," she added with a croak, her throat raw and as hot as the Sahara Desert.

Someone jammed a needle into her left arm and she winced. She hated needles. Her frown deepened. *Why* did she hate needles?

She fought down a sense of panic as voices she couldn't decipher rose around her. She looked up at the prime male specimen again. "What happened?" she asked in the croaky voice only a bullfrog would envy.

"You'll be fine." His lips curved into a smile and those eyes the color of blue topaz filled with a reassurance she wasn't exactly buying. She didn't feel fine. She felt as if her body was on fire.

"What's your last name, Maggie?" he asked, smoothing her hair away from her face with a tenderness that felt almost foreign to her. Now why was that? she wondered.

Her vision blurred again until there were two of her angels of mercy gazing down at her with concern banked in their heavenly eyes. Her world started to fade to a dark murky gray, then quickly to black seconds after she whispered, "I was hoping you could tell me."

As HE'D DONE every day for the last six, Cale Perry pulled his Dodge Ram pickup into the visitors' parking lot of the UCLA Medical Center. He avoided the emergency access where everyone knew him and opted for the anonymity of the main entrance. Holding a brown paper bag that was giving off the tantalizing aroma of fried foods, he sauntered through the automatic sliding glass doors, a tuneless whistle on his lips. After a quick scan of the corridor for familiar faces, he slipped into the elevator, where he pushed the button for the fourth floor.

He hadn't told a soul where he'd been disappearing to once his shift ended, especially not his nosy brothers, Drew and Ben, or Tilly Jensen, a family friend and E.R. nurse, who happened to be on duty the night of Maggie's accident. They'd never understand the inexplicable need that drove him to the hospital on a nightly basis, and they most certainly couldn't possibly understand how Cale felt drawn to Maggie. In fact, about the only thing he did know was that she needed him, and that alone was reason enough for him.

Where she came from or why she'd been trapped in a burning paint-supply warehouse were as much a mystery to her as they were to Cale, not to mention to the cops or the arson investigation team. The way he figured it, there were a lot of blank spaces in Maggie's memory, and he couldn't find a single, solitary reason why he should not be the one to help her fill in those gaps.

A rueful grin slid across his lips when the doors opened on the fourth floor of the medical center. If his brothers found out he was acting out yet another knight-in-shining-armor fantasy over a woman he didn't know they'd never let him hear the end of it.

He turned left when he got off the elevator and nodded to the medical staff huddled around the nurses' station as he made his way toward the rooms at the end of the long corridor. Without a doubt, his brothers would most definitely think him crazy, and in all honesty, they were probably right. There wasn't much information on his mystery woman, except that her eyes were an intriguing combination of blue, green and gold. Her hair, a shimmering shade of cinnamon, hung halfway down her back in long, soft waves, and she had a serious penchant for junk food. A petite thing, she had plenty of curves to heighten any man's interest, along with a sweet, lyrical voice that had returned once the effects of the smoke inhalation had dissipated. She had a disposition to match, as well. Considering her past remained unknown, he thought her attitude admirable.

For reasons that defied every known source of logic he'd reviewed and subsequently discounted since he'd first found Maggie With-No-Last-Name surrounded by gallons and gallons of paint cans inside the burning warehouse, he was more than intrigued by this mysterious stranger who stirred his blood and fired his imagination.

He'd stayed with her in the hospital that first night. His shift had ended, so he'd just...stayed. At first he'd told himself it was only because she'd asked him to— a desperate plea that had tugged at his heart. It hadn't been the first time a victim he'd treated on the scene had wanted him to stay. Until Maggie, he'd always just assured them the doctors would take good care of them, then left without a backward glance. But something in her voice, something he couldn't quite define, had pulled at him hard. In the end, he simply couldn't leave her.

The next day his tendency toward heroism faded

into worry for one simple reason—he hadn't been able to get Maggie out of his mind.

Because this one victim out of the thousands he'd treated since becoming a paramedic six years ago had caught him off guard and touched an emotional chord he'd kept carefully hidden, he'd been more than a little alarmed. Maggie was sweet, pretty and scared, however, so what guy wouldn't feel like a knight on a white charger?

The next day he brought in a motorcycle rider who'd been involved in a collision and damned if Cale didn't act like a fool by asking the E.R. doc who had treated Maggie about her condition. Mere curiosity, he'd told himself over and over once he'd left with his partner, Brady Kent.

Until his shift had ended, and he'd driven straight to the hospital.

Curiosity and his arguments of "it's only mild concern" flew out the window when he'd walked into her room. His heart had slammed into his rib cage when she'd looked over at him and offered a weak, morphine-induced smile.

He'd pulled up a chair and had sat with her that night, and every night since, waiting until she'd fallen asleep before finally going home to his small house near the beach. Getting to know Maggie wasn't exactly the easiest thing he'd ever done considering her past remained elusive, but Cale knew enough about her personality to be highly intrigued and maybe even a little bewitched.

Now, he couldn't seem to stay away from her.

He pushed through the door to Maggie's room, the

tuneless whistle stilling on his lips. She glanced his way from her hospital bed, her eyes a piercing shade of blue rimmed in gold. With her mouth set in a grim line, she didn't look at all pleased to see him.

He stepped into the room and quickly realized she wasn't alone. He easily pegged the two gentlemen dressed in suits as cops. One stood at the foot of the bed, while the other leaned casually with one shoulder braced against the wall closest to the window overlooking the parking lot.

The older of the two detectives shot him a dark look. "You'll have to come back later," he told Cale without moving from his stance near the window.

Maggie shifted her attention to the detective. "He'll be staying," she replied. Her firm and somewhat harsh tone took Cale by surprise. The Maggie he knew was sweet and soft-spoken. Obviously there was more to his mystery woman than met the eye.

The younger detective looked Cale up and down. "You a lawyer?"

Cale approached Maggie and set the grease-stained bag on the tall metal nightstand. "No. A friend," he answered cautiously. "Is there a problem, detective?"

Being a paramedic, he came in contact with law enforcement practically on a daily basis, however most of his experiences were either with the uniformed cops or the guys in the arson unit within the fire department.

Maggie let out a huff of breath. "I already told you. I must've lost my purse in the fire. I don't have any identification."

"How is it you know Ms...." The detective glanced in Maggie's direction. "Ms. Doe?" he finished, his gaze skeptical.

She looked at Cale. "What Detective Villanueva is trying to ask is if you know who I am. Isn't that right, Detective?"

"What's going on here?" Cale demanded, feeling his protective instincts rise to the surface.

"We're only trying to determine why Ms. Doe was at the Harrison Paint and Wallpaper warehouse. Alone. Especially since the warehouse was closed, not to mention that it isn't open to the general public."

The color in Maggie's eyes brightened considerably. "I already told you, I don't know anything."

"How convenient," Villanueva muttered.

"Until my memory returns, I'm afraid I won't be of much assistance to you."

The older, stout detective near the window straightened and gave his partner a quick glance, motioning toward the door with a nod of his head. "You have my card," he said. "In case you remember anything."

Cale waited for them to leave before turning his attention back to Maggie. "What was that about?"

Maggie straightened the already perfectly arranged bed covers. "Exactly what they said. They want to know why I was in the warehouse. I'd like to know, as well."

The question had crossed Cale's mind, too, more than once. He also understood that Maggie had spoken the truth when she'd told the detectives that until her memory returned, she'd have no answers, only questions of her own.

"They don't believe me," she said abruptly. "Who can blame them, really? I sound like something out of a bad soap opera."

Despite the hint of truth to her statement, Cale chuckled lightly as he carried the visitor's chair closer to the bed. "I thought the truth was supposed to be stranger than fiction."

She looked over at him, her eyebrows suddenly pulled down into a frown. Whatever was on her mind, she kept it to herself. After a brief moment, she shook her head then graced him with a hint of a smile. Her pert little nose twitched, as if she were a bunny rabbit anticipating the delightful feast of an unguarded vegetable garden. "Is that a cheeseburger?"

His heart stuttered at the pure pleasure softening her features. "The lady knows her junk food."

"I can't believe you remembered," she said in the same soft voice that had been haunting his dreams all week.

The awe in her voice had him wondering why something so trivial as a cheeseburger brought her such delight. Almost as if no one had ever done anything as ordinary as bring her a special treat. He'd ask her about it, but she'd only whisper, "I don't know," and then her eyes would cloud with worry or frustration.

He reached across the bed to settle his hand over her fingers peeking out from the cast that extended to her elbow. Her skin was soft, smooth and silky. If her fingers were this soft, he'd surely drive himself insane imagining the feel of the rest of her body.

"You said it was your favorite."

Her grin widened, and she playfully snatched the bag from his hands. "I might not know much about who I am, where I belong or what I was doing in a burning warehouse but I most assuredly know a cheeseburger and fries when I smell them."

Cale chuckled again despite the frightening truth of her statement. Where *did* she belong? The absence of a ring on her left finger, or of the pale circle caused by wearing one for any length of time, might indicate she didn't have a husband in the picture, but it didn't alleviate the possibility of a boyfriend or a serious relationship. The doctors had told her she'd never had any children, but she'd merely shrugged and muttered they no doubt knew more than she.

According to Maggie, the psychiatrist who came to see her on a daily basis had told her she was suffering from level III amnesia, which was generally caused by medical trauma. Well, she'd certainly had that, Cale thought, watching her carefully unwrap the cheeseburger with her good hand. In addition to a broken wrist, smoke inhalation and enough bruises to play connect-the-dots, she'd suffered a severe concussion when a shelf filled with paint cans had fallen on top of her.

She took a bite of the burger, closed her eyes and issued a sultry little moan of pleasure.

Cale exhaled slowly as his imagination took flight. "I take it the lady is pleased." He leaned back in the chair and propped his foot over his knee, which did nothing to lessen the snug fit of his jeans.

A brief nod followed another bite before she finally answered him. "Very pleased. This is the best thing that's happened to me all day."

"I know those detectives must've been rough on you, but they're only doing their job."

She sighed and set the rest of the burger down on the wheeled table as if her appetite had vanished. He took the action as warning sign of impending not-so-good news.

She dropped her gaze to the cast on her right arm. "That's not what I meant. A social worker came to see me today," she said quietly.

"And?" he prompted.

She pulled in a deep breath and let it out slowly before she looked over at him. That same desperation he'd seen the night of the explosion, along with a dose of panic, returned. "And they're releasing me tomorrow. Mrs. Sutter suggested I consider going to a long-term care facility."

He straightened, alarm rippling through him. "Why?" he demanded. He'd been around the medical profession long enough to know *long-term care* was code for nursing home. Because of Maggie's inability to remember anything about herself, it wouldn't be all that unusual for her to be transferred to a psych hospital. The thought of Maggie in an understaffed, state-operated facility filled him with more dread than he imagined possible.

She made an attempt to cross her arms over her chest, but the weight of the cast and the cumbersome

IV line had her frowning instead. "Because," she said, dropping her hands to her lap, "I don't know who I am or where I live. It doesn't appear so far that anyone is looking for me, either, since the detectives informed me they had no missing persons report on file for anyone fitting my description. The social worker said I should consider her suggestion, since, according to her, I'm relatively incapable of taking care of myself."

From what Cale had witnessed upon entering her room, she could take care of herself just fine. There had to be something he could do to help her. So what if he felt himself slipping into a time-honored tradition? He'd been lending a helping hand to others for as long as he cared to remember. Granted, he'd been making a concentrated effort of late to be a little more discriminate, but Maggie honestly needed a champion. Until she regained her memory, she had no one else. Besides, he hardly believed helping Maggie would result in him having to change his telephone number again or require him to obtain a restraining order, the way he had when Paulette Johnson had become a little too clingy.

"What about fingerprints?" he asked. The authorities had taken her prints in an attempt to identify her. "Haven't you heard anything?"

Disappointment filled her gaze. "According to Mrs. Sutter, nothing showed up. She also said it's not all that unusual. I've just probably never been fingerprinted for anything."

He slid his hand over hers again. "Hey, look at the bright side. At least you're not a criminal."

The look she gave him momentarily startled him. Cold and icy, and not the Maggie he'd come to know the past few days.

"Maybe I've just never been caught."

Cale didn't think so. He'd seen and treated enough of the criminal element in Los Angeles to know the difference. Maggie's identity might be unknown, but that she was a criminal wasn't even a remote possibility in his mind.

"Can you?" he asked. "Take care of yourself, I mean?"

Slowly, she pulled her hand from beneath his. "I know red means stop and green means go." Anger and frustration lined her voice, and the gold rim surrounding her irises brightened. "I know fire is hot and ice is cold. If it's raining, take an umbrella. If the telephone rings, answer it. I know what day it is, the month and even the year. I think I can cook, and I know how to make change so I can at least buy my meals if I can't."

Cale shrugged. "Then what's the problem?"

"I don't know where I live or even how I make my living. Since I don't know if I have any family or anywhere to go, Mrs. Sutter explained a long-term care facility would at least assume my care until I'm better equipped to do so myself."

"What if..." He stopped and carefully considered his next words. Once uttered, he couldn't take them back. But, dammit, he just didn't have the heart to turn his back on someone who really needed him.

"What if you had someone willing to take care of you?" he blurted before he could change his mind.

She tilted her head slightly, and frowned. "What do you mean?"

His brothers were right. He *was* crazy. Not to mention so far out of control his common sense had deserted him...again.

*She's not like the others,* his conscience rallied. Or was that his libido talking? Did it really matter? He didn't think so.

"What if you had someone willing to see to it that you're safe?" There. He'd said it. No taking the words back now.

"I don't know anyone." She blinked back the moisture suddenly shining in her eyes. "I don't know *anything*," she said, her voice tight.

"Tell this Sutter woman *I'll* care for you." The ground slipped out from under him as he stepped off the cliff into a sea of insanity. His own history with the opposite sex should have had him running in the opposite direction. But how could he turn his back on Maggie when she needed him the most?

He couldn't. And that's when the trouble always started.

Her smile was thin as she swiped at the tears with her good hand. "That's very sweet of you, Cale. But it still doesn't solve my problem. Besides, what if Mrs. Sutter decided to check on me."

He had his doubts on that score. "So what if she does? In any case, it'll never happen. The heavy caseload of the social system in this county prohibits extravagances. The social workers spend their time on only the most severe cases, and, Maggie, you hardly qualify as a severe case."

*Slow Burn*

He reached across the bed and grabbed her hand again. He wanted to do more than hold her hand, he wanted to gather her in his arms and hold her close, promise her everything would be okay in the end. It didn't matter that her future was uncertain. The urge to comfort her was strong, just as strong as the need to feel her soft curves pressed against him.

He smoothed his thumb over her slender fingers. "You call Mrs. Sutter and tell her you've got a place to go tomorrow when they release you, and that'll be the end of it. You can stay at my place for as long as you need."

She snatched her hand away. "No—"

"Just until you get your memory back." He moved from the chair and sat next to her on the edge of the bed. He braced his hands on the mattress to bracket her hips, his body stirring at the closeness. Momentarily distracted by the shape of her mouth, he simply stared.

"I couldn't," she said, but she didn't sound convincing.

"Yes, you can. Look, aren't your doctors saying it could only be a few days until your memory returns? Do you really want to go to a long-term care facility?"

She shook her head, and a hank of fiery hair fell over her shoulder. The wavy ends teased the slope of her breasts beneath the cotton hospital gown. "Or maybe a few weeks, or months, or even never. You've already been so kind to me, Cale. I won't ask any more of you."

"You aren't asking," he argued. "I'm offering."

He understood her fear, or at least he liked to think

he did. The truth wasn't that simple. He couldn't begin to imagine what it would be like not to know where he came from or the members of his own family. Of course, when his brothers learned he'd brought home a total stranger, they'd be convinced he'd taken leave of his common sense for sure this time.

Where Maggie was concerned, they were probably right. Didn't he have enough disastrous relationships in his past to prove their arguments? Okay, so maybe there was some truth here. But, none of those women was Maggie. She genuinely needed his help. He wasn't offering a permanent solution, only a temporary one.

"Cases that last that long are the exception, Maggie, not the rule," he said gently.

"I don't know..."

"Come stay with me, just until we can figure out where you really belong. I've got a quiet little place near the beach and a bedroom to spare. You'll be perfectly safe there, and it's a hell of a lot better than some sterile environment where you'll just be another name on a chart."

"I might not even live in L.A.," she argued. "Or California for that matter. Maybe I was just passing through and was in the wrong place at the wrong time. Or maybe I was visiting someone."

"Then why hasn't anyone else come to see you? And why wasn't anyone else at the scene when we found you?"

She dropped her head back against the pillow and

closed her eyes, but not before he saw defeat pass through them.

"It'll give you a quiet, peaceful place to recuperate and when I'm off duty, maybe I can help you find out who you really are."

She opened her eyes. "But...how can I?" she asked, her voice barely above a whisper. "You're a complete stranger. I don't even know you."

"You don't even know yourself at this point," he said dryly.

"Exactly." She sat up again. "What if I'm a serial killer or something equally horrible? How do you know I won't rob you blind? You wouldn't even know who to tell the police to arrest."

Cale chuckled. "The perfect crime."

"It's not funny."

Lifting his hand, he gently smoothed his knuckles over her satiny cheek. "What other choice do you have, Maggie? It's either me or a state facility."

"You're not giving me much by way of options, are you?"

"You don't *have* a lot of options," he said truthfully, lowering his hand. "It's me or the funny farm, babe."

"I don't think I'm used to being told what to do." She shot him a frustrated glance. "Because I sure don't like it now."

# 2

*SHE WORE BLACK. Simple. Basic. Elegant. Of course for a woman in her line of work, black was always the most appropriate color. She considered it her signature color, with one small exception—the red silk hankie with an embroidered V done in an elegant, delicate script. She preferred to think of it as her calling card.*

*She pretended mild interest as her bore of a host preened over his most prized possession: a priceless, yet little-known Carracci painting he'd presumably acquired at an estate auction...or so he claimed. She knew better. The Carracci failed to garner her attention, for now. There was only one reason she was in Rome, and it had zilch to do with priceless art.*

*Slowly and deliberately, she slid her hand over his arm in an unmistakable gesture. He had what she wanted, and before the night drew to a close, she'd have what she came for...*

MAGGIE AWOKE with a start, heart pounding, breathing ragged. The thin cotton hospital gown clung to her sweat-moistened body as she struggled to recall the details of the dream. She wasn't sure what it all meant, but she suspected there was some clue to her identity attempting to rise to the surface.

Not just her identity, she thought, pulling in a deep breath that did little to calm her, but her life.

Who was she? Where did she come from? And more importantly, what exactly did she do for a living? From the misty visions of the dream, she almost dreaded the answer.

A quick glance at the clock on the wall next to the television reminded her that Cale would be arriving to take her home shortly. Not home exactly, but away from the hospital and the threat of the unknown. He really was angel. What kind of guy took in not just a total stranger, but someone who didn't even know herself. Obviously, Cale was one of the good guys, and for reasons she had no nope of comprehending at the moment, she wasn't exactly comfortable with the idea. It wasn't that she didn't feel an enormous amount of gratitude for his unconditional generosity, but what if the nagging sensation in the back of her mind was true? What if she wasn't what he believed her to be, just some poor schmuck in the wrong place at the wrong time? The dream...

"No," she said in a firm tone. She *had* to stop thinking about it, or she'd end up with another one of those horrendous headaches again, the kind that had sledgehammers, jackhammers and a cacophony of chain saws all vying to be the loudest. The doctors may have told her not to force her memory, but in her opinion, that was easy for them to say. What were *their* chances of getting lost in their own neighborhoods?

She sat up and cautiously swung her feet over the side of the bed to the small footstool. Following a breakfast of stale toast, saltless scrambled eggs and cold coffee, the morning nurse had removed her IV as promised, eliminating at least one cumbersome attachment. Unfortunately, the cast on her right arm wouldn't be so easily discarded, at least for another six to eight weeks while her wrist healed. One thing she had learned about herself, she most assuredly was right-handed.

The call she'd placed to the social worker had been simple. As Cale predicted, all Mrs. Sutter had asked for had been an address and telephone number in case she needed to contact her. The call to Detective Villanueva had been relatively painless, as well, except his coolness made her uncomfortable. Still, he'd thanked her for the call and promised to be in touch, which sounded more like a threat than an offer of assistance.

She pressed the button to turn on the television to a cable news network for background noise. While the reports of current events were vaguely familiar to her, none of the clips that flashed across the screen of the various cities through the U.S. gave so much as a tiny nudge to her absent memory. She did recognize certain landmarks and buildings from New York City and Chicago. Independence Hall in Philadelphia and the Kodak Theater in Hollywood were both familiar sights when she spotted them in a couple of tourism commercials. An advertisement for Disneyland didn't hold any special meaning or spark a single memory of childhood. She just *knew* of these places, the way she knew the succession of color in a rainbow or the caloric difference between chocolate cake and a granola bar, and which of the two she preferred.

In a determined effort to stop stressing herself into another migraine, she shoved her encased arm into the plastic bag and used the white medical tape the nurse had left her so she could seal the bag closed around her cast, hoping to make it watertight. Moving slowly, she managed to make her way across the room to the bathroom she shared with the patient in the next room. She wasn't setting any speed records, that was for sure, but at least she was able to shower and wash her hair, albeit awkwardly. Drying herself off wasn't quite the sideshow she'd expected, and she'd even managed to apply lotion to most of her body.

Cale had thoughtfully brought her some clothes to wear since her own had been ruined. He'd proven quite resourceful, too, checking her tattered garments for the right sizes. His choices left little to be desired, but a woman in her situation had no room for complaints, especially since he'd footed the bill. She'd made him give her the receipt and as soon as she found a job, or better yet, herself, she'd pay back every cent.

She slipped into a pair of panties and tried not to think about Cale purchasing something so intimate for her. A blush stained her cheeks even though the plain white cotton panties to match the plain white cotton bra didn't exactly scream *sexy*. She didn't know whether she had Cale or a saleswoman to thank for the thigh-high comfort of the panties, but as she stared at the freshly laundered, button-fly jeans, she couldn't help wondering what on earth he'd been thinking.

She stepped into the heavy denim and pulled them up her legs without too much trouble. Before even fastening them she knew they'd be a comfortable fit, but the dancing around on her toes as she struggled with each button had her not only breaking out in a sweat, but near tears. As much as she appreciated his thoughtfulness, couldn't he have brought her some leggings or even a pair of sweats? She'd be happy with a pair of pull-on pants made by Poly and Ester, the tacky fabric twins, just so she could avoid buttons, snaps or zippers.

Dammit, she would *not* cry. She'd been doing far too much of that lately.

She sat on the edge of the commode to catch her breath and stared at the bra on the little stool next to the shower as if it were a two-headed snake. With nothing else to do but try, she reached for the bra and entered a new realm of humiliation. Slipping her arms through the shoulder straps and hooking the back was out of the question, so she decided to put the evil contraption on backwards, fasten the ends together in front, then twist it around her body.

After several failed attempts, her stern lectures about not crying came back to taunt her as her eyes filled with more tears of frustration. There was no way around it. She'd have to swallow her pride and ring the nurse for assistance.

Her hand stilled over the little pull chain in the small, semiprivate bathroom when she heard the door to her room open. "Nurse?" she called out in relief. "If you have a minute, I could really use your help."

Without a sound, the heavy door swung open. Maggie gasped when she turned to find Cale instead of the nurse she'd been expecting.

His expression instantly shifted from concern to desire right before her eyes. The man was definitely good for her ego. Not five seconds ago she'd managed to convince herself she looked like an idiot incapable of doing something as simple as buttoning up a pair of Levi's. Now she was only behaving like one as she stood and stared at him, shocked into utter silence by the not-unpleasant sensation of warmth uncurling in her belly and spreading outward with languid heat through her limbs.

He cleared his throat. "Excuse me," he murmured as he spun around quickly to allow her a modicum of privacy.

Still feeling decidedly confused and definitely aroused by her reaction to him, she made a hasty grab for the towel she'd tossed on the edge of the sink earlier. With a hard snap, she swung her cast against the white porcelain. Tears sprang to her eyes as pain shot up her arm. She reached blindly for the wall to steady herself, but instead of touching the cool ceramic tile, her good hand came in contact with a solid wall of masculinity.

His arms were around her, steadying her and holding her close. *Don't cry*, she thought.

But one whispered word of comfort, one large male hand gliding over the exposed skin of her back in a gentle, soothing motion, and tears of pain and frustration poured from her eyes like a busted water main.

"It'll get better, Maggie. I promise you, it will."

She pulled back slightly to look up at him. "How can you say that?" she asked around a sob. "You know as much about me as I do, and we're not talking a wealth of knowledge here, either."

His incredible smile was as kind as the expression that softened his intense blue eyes. "You're in pain." He slid the pad of his thumb across her cheek to dry her tears. "I'll call the nurse."

The tenderness he showed her stirred something deep inside her, a wealth of emotion she had no hope of truly understanding until she acquired at least some recollection of her past as a comparison.

She sniffled and shook her head. What she really wanted to do was scream. Between her faulty gray matter and the delicious tingling sprinting through her body, she figured she was more than a little entitled.

No doubt she was suffering with some twisted version of Stockholm Syndrome. Cale might not be her captor, but she had come to depend on him, if only slightly. Although she'd actually started looking forward to his nightly visits, that little piece of reality saddened her. Did she really have no other person in her life that cared about her? Wasn't there someone, somewhere, missing her? Parents, grandparents, an uncle or an aunt? What about siblings, an employer? A cat or a pair of goldfish?

She pulled in a steadying breath only to be swamped by the unique scent she'd come to associate with Cale. That sensual blend of spice and pure male any woman in her right mind, or not as her case might be, would have difficulty resisting.

She used the edge of the towel clutched to her chest to dry her eyes. "My mind is foggy enough." She managed what she hoped was a brave smile and tried not to think about that musky, masculine scent giving her most feminine senses a sharp jolt. "Adding pain-killers to the confusion is the last thing I need."

He didn't look that convinced. "You were calling the nurse for a reason."

Keeping the towel clutched to her chest, she took a step back. "I needed assistance."

"Assistance...?" he prompted.

She let out a sigh. "Yes. With getting dressed." Her gaze dipped pointedly to the bra lying on the tiled floor at her feet.

A questioning frown tugged his eyebrows low over his eyes a half second before they arched upward as realization dawned. "Ah," he said. That killer smile returned to his handsome face, kicking her pulse rate up a couple of notches.

He stooped to pick up the bra and handed it to her. "Slip into it and I'll fasten it for you."

With the bra dangling from her fingertips, she stared at Cale in fascination. He couldn't seriously be offering his services for something so...so intimate, could he? Maybe she shouldn't be surprised. After all, the man hadn't only offered a total stranger a place to live, he'd bought clothes for her to wear and had even gone to the trouble of digging through her ruined garments to find out her sizes.

He turned around and stood with his back to her, giving her a sense of privacy. If she refused, she'd feel petty and foolish. The man wasn't making a pass at her. He was offering to help her dress since she obviously couldn't do it for herself. There wasn't anything sexual about it. Well...hardly anything sexual about it.

She turned her back to him, dropped the towel and slipped into the bra. Holding the cups awkwardly in place, she said, "Okay."

The first brush of his fingers against her sides as he took hold of the ends of the bra nearly had her jumping out of her skin. His touch was gentle and completely impersonal as he worked the fasteners, but that didn't stop a delightful shiver from glancing down her spine.

He reached around her and bent to snag the navy-blue cotton top from the stool. "Arms up," he ordered.

Oh, no. This part she could handle on her own. She took the top from him, knowing she'd go just a little more nuts if he put his hands on her body again. "Thank you," she said, "but I think I can take it from here."

"I'll wait outside." With one last look, he quietly closed the bathroom door behind him. Alone, she couldn't stop the smile from spreading across her lips at the obvious disappointment in his gaze.

Once she'd finished dressing, she took a moment to check her appearance in the mirror. She might not know who she was or where she came from, but there was one thing she understood completely—sexual chemistry and attraction, especially since her hormones went into overtime whenever Cale was around.

CALE KNEW trouble when he saw it, and trouble definitely had arrived in his life in the form of the mysterious Maggie with her sexy little smile, eyes that changed color with her mood and rich cinnamon hair that had his fingers itching to touch the silky strands. Those reddish-brown tresses weren't the only thing soft about her, either. His testosterone had shot through the roof for those few seconds his fingers had brushed against her silky skin.

He added a new shade of eye color to his list, too. Turquoise—the color of Maggie's eyes when she was aroused. Always one of his favorites, this particular shade ranked at the top of his list, especially since he knew without a doubt he was solely responsible for it.

He paced around the hospital room while he waited for her to emerge from the bathroom. Like his brothers, he was no stranger to relationships, although he did like to think his held at least a modicum of meaning in comparison.

His little brother, Drew, hardly ever dated the same woman more than three times. In fact, Drew gave new meaning to the term *little black book*. He had more of a big black binder. He wasn't cruel, and he never led a woman on, but no one doubted Drew's bedroom did indeed boast a revolving door.

As for his older brother, other than a few short-term relationships, Ben tended to steer clear of the opposite sex. Or more accurately, Cale thought, from any form of relationship that remotely resembled a serious or lasting affair.

By comparison, Cale figured he was the most normal of the three. At least he dated. He even had relationships that lasted longer than a week, which was more than he could say for Drew. To his way of thinking, taking the time to get to know a woman was all a part of the fun. For him, there was something satisfying about unraveling all those intimate secrets and feminine mysteries.

So maybe that had something to do with his interest and attraction to Maggie, because she absolutely had plenty of mystery. Sure, his brothers would no doubt consider her another of his damsels in distress; the woman had more secrets than the CIA. But she needed his help, not just in offering her a place to live, but in rediscovering her past. So what if he'd known her less than a week and already was more than intrigued by her? Was it his fault she was sweet and feisty, a combination he found incredibly sexy and damned hard to resist?

She was tiny, almost helpless at first appearance, but he'd seen her handle her own against those two surly detectives last night. And although her situation indicated otherwise, he'd hardly slap a weak or dependent label on her. In fact, *stubborn* and *determined* applied to her all too well, telling him whether she knew it or not, Maggie wasn't just a fighter, but a survivor, as well.

Oh, yeah. Maggie was a mystery all right, but an exciting one. And he'd always been a sucker for a little excitement, not to mention a good mystery, even if he did know what his family would have to say about it.

Ever since he was a kid he'd collected strays. He didn't need another two-hundred-dollar-an-hour shrink to warn him he was about to repeat the pattern all over again. Although, even he had to admit, sparrows that had fallen from their nest were a hell of a lot more innocuous than a living, breathing woman without a past. But he'd been saving lives ever since his mother had died in the line of duty when he was only eight years old. He couldn't very well change now. To his way of thinking, there was nothing wrong with being a nurturer. In fact, it had made his becoming a paramedic the obvious career choice.

Okay, so this time he didn't have a bird with a broken wing that needed to be cared for until it healed. Maggie wasn't an abandoned kitten, but she did need his help. He wasn't the kind of guy to turn his back on something—or someone—in their hour of need.

Besides, he reasoned, weren't his strays always placed in good homes eventually? Okay, except for Pogo, the three-legged dog he'd rescued from a beating by the mean old SOB who had lived in his childhood neighborhood. The dog had been of such mixed heritage, even the vet had been hard-pressed to put a breed label on the poor mutt. It hadn't mattered to Cale. He and Pogo had remained inseparable until the day the old dog had finally passed on, shortly after Cale graduated high school.

Maybe if he had listened to the psychobabble of the child psychologist who'd treated him and his brothers when their father had died shortly after their mother, he might be a little worried about taking a stranger into his home. He wasn't helping Maggie because of some misguided or misplaced need to save the world because he hadn't been able to save his mother or even his father. He really wasn't. Maggie needed someone, even if she did jump-start his libido with a simple little smile or a teary-eyed, gratitude-filled look in her intriguing eyes.

He stopped his pacing when the bathroom door finally opened and Maggie walked into the sterile hospital room. His breathing nearly halted, as well, or was that his heart that had stopped beating?

He couldn't be sure, mainly because he couldn't help staring at the way the dark-blue denim clung enticingly to her legs and outlined the gentle swell of her hips. She approached the metal nightstand and bent over to peer into the drawer. The sight of her curvy backside had him struggling for breath again.

"I'll be ready in a sec," she said, tossing the few personal items into the white plastic bag the hospital had provided.

His vocal chords refused to function, and all he could manage was a brief nod of his head. His gaze zeroed in on the lightweight fabric of the plain cotton top as it hugged her very full breasts and outlined her slender waist, leaving him with an almost uncontrollable urge to slip his hand beneath the serviceable fabric and explore every inch of her skin.

Oh, yeah. Cale Perry knew trouble when it saw it, all right. And her name was Maggie.

# 3

FROM THE passenger seat of Cale's red four-wheel-drive pickup, Maggie watched the passing scenery along Ocean Boulevard. Regardless of how thin a chance, she'd still hoped something—a building, a tree, maybe even a street sign or billboard—would pull her memory out of hiding.

"Nothing is familiar," she told Cale as he came to a stop behind a line of cars waiting for the traffic light to turn green.

He glanced her way, then took her by surprise when he reached across the bench seat to slip his hand over hers, as if touching her was something he did all the time. Her body said otherwise. When he gave her hand a reassuring squeeze, delightful little shockwaves traveled up her arm and shot straight to the tips of her breasts with electrifying accuracy.

"Did you expect otherwise?" he asked, his voice one of concern, not lust.

Too bad.

"Hoped is more like it." She removed her hand from beneath his to slip a nonexistent stray lock of hair behind her ear. She didn't think she was unaccustomed to being touched, which left only one other option. Her desire for physical distance, however

minute, stemmed from something much more basic...like an inexplicable sexual attraction to a total
stranger. Her life, such as it was, was complicated
enough and she should definitely not compound her
problems by allowing her hormones to run amuck.
Just because her guide in an unfamiliar world was
sexier than any man had a right to be, and was able to
make her breath still with one slanted look or a gentle
touch, did *not* put him on her agenda.

Cale turned his attention back to the road and
moved forward with the rest of the traffic. "You're
not supposed to force your memories. When your
memory does return, it'll be in its own time."

She let out a sigh and looked out the window
again. "I know." She might not like it, but Cale was
right. He only repeated what the doctors had been
telling her for the last few days. Still, it unnerved her
that he appeared to possess an uncanny ability to
read her mind. An interesting concept, she mused,
since her mind was pretty much a blank page.

At least she was out of the hospital and not in a
long-term care facility. No matter how diplomatic
Mrs. Sutter had been in her explanation, the place
she'd described had just screamed loony bin. Maggie
wasn't crazy or even mentally incompetent, she just
didn't know her identity.

"I can't thank you enough for everything you've
done," she blurted, anxious for a break from her own
morose thoughts. "I'm not even sure how to begin to
repay you."

Just as she realized exactly what she'd implied, he
glanced her way again. Surely she didn't imagine the

way his gaze swept over her. Only her own twisted imagination could spark the dozen or so lurid images running through her mind with the speed of light. Her throat should never have felt drier than dust, either, and her pulse rate couldn't have increased. But she'd felt every ounce of those tell-tale physiological changes in her body, just because she'd *imagined* Cale looking at her with blatant male appreciation in his gaze. At least that was her argument, until she witnessed the adorable grin that tugged his lips and deepened the laugh lines surrounding his eyes. At that moment, she knew it hadn't been her imagination, just as she knew the sudden acceleration of her heartbeat was as real as it got.

"There's no thanks necessary." He shifted his attention back to the road. "If you can cook, that'll be payment enough. I get kinda tired of my own cooking."

A wry grin touched her lips. "I guess we'll have to see, won't we?"

She didn't feel completely comfortable intruding on Cale's life, but as he'd so eloquently stated, it was either him or the funny farm. By accepting his very generous offer, she'd be free to come and go as she pleased, and she hoped to find out a thing or two or three about her past. So what if she'd have to leave the proverbial trail of bread crumbs to find her way home again? At least she had freedom, and that had to count for something.

Shortly after they entered the city limits of Hermosa Beach, Cale took a left off Ocean Boulevard into a residential district, which brought them even closer to the shores of the Pacific Ocean. After several more turns, Cale slowed and pulled into a sloped drive-way, parking in front of a two-car garage with a roll-up door painted a hideous shade of turquoise.

Above the garage was the house, in a much more pleasing-to-the-eye shade of dove-gray siding, how-ever, the trim and the concrete staircase leading up to the house were the same garish color as the garage door. Flanking the driveway were two planters made of railroad ties. They were filled with shrubs in dire need of TLC before they completely lost the battle be-ing pitifully waged against a determined army of dandelions.

"It's a work in progress," Cale said with a nod to-ward the house.

She glanced around the area. The well-kept homes only yards from the beach, whether modest in size or more elaborate and ornate, spoke of prime real estate. "Nice neighborhood."

Cale chuckled. "Don't be too impressed. I pull in a decent salary, but not enough to afford something like this on my own. Thanks to my aunt, the lawyers handling my folks' probate set up a trust fund for me and my brothers."

So he had family. She wondered what these broth-ers of his would say about her living with Cale, albeit temporarily. If she'd brought home a total stranger…

If she'd brought home a total stranger—what? The answer faded away into the misty remnants of her mind before she had a chance to catch it, filling her with renewed frustration.

Cale snagged the plastic bag containing her few

personal items before opening the door to the truck. The soothing scent of the sea instantly slipped inside. She pulled in a deep breath and waited, hoping for another spark of some distant memory, only to be further disappointed. Somehow she *knew* the sea comforted her. She only wished she knew why.

With yet another gusty sigh, she opened her door and slid from the truck to follow Cale up the turquoise steps. "What did your parents do?" she asked, as he slipped the key into the lock.

He looked back at her before pushing open the door. There was no mistaking the hint of sadness in his eyes. "They were both firefighters." Had he been a child when his parents had passed away? Could that be why he'd taken her in so easily, because he had firsthand experience of suddenly finding himself alone in the world?

Before she could ask him, he abruptly changed the subject. "I hope you like animals," he said as he opened the door.

No fear climbed up her spine at the thought of facing an animal, so she simply shrugged and followed Cale inside. The sound of clicking toenails on a newly finished hardwood floor greeted them and they were met by a very large, furry black dog of an indeterminate breed. The dog jumped around Cale, filled with excitement.

"Maggie, meet Pearl." To the dog he said, "You be a good girl."

Pearl immediately sat, tongue lolling out of her mouth with an expectant look in her enormous brown eyes as she stared at Maggie.

She took a hesitant step forward, her left hand extended for Pearl to sniff. Instead of a cold nose, a warm tongue lapped at her hand. Pearl's oddly short bushy tail polished the floor with record speed.

"Oh, she's sweet," Maggie said, smiling up at Cale. That look was in his eyes again, the one that held a combination of awe and desire. Her pulse revved again. Needing a moment to remind herself that feeling all warm and fuzzy inside was not the wisest course, she flipped her attention back to Pearl. The canine's lips were pulled back as she showed off a set of lethal-looking teeth.

"I don't think she likes me," she said, unsure whether or not to take a giant step backward.

Cale chuckled. "Of course she does."

Maggie pasted a smile on her face and hoped the dog took it as a sign of friendship. "Then why is she snarling at me?"

"She's not snarling, she's smiling."

Maggie frowned. "Excuse me?" Dogs did not *smile,* that much she did know.

"Smiling." Cale closed the door and set the bag next to a lamp on a rustic pine sofa table nestled against the wall nearest the door. "She does it all the time when she's happy."

Maggie eyed the dog cautiously and slowly bent down to rub her chest. Pearl's "grin" widened and her eyes took on a glazed look of deep pleasure. "And here I thought dogs only wagged their tails to show their emotions."

"She's kind of unique that way." Cale cleared his

throat and headed into the kitchen. "Want something to drink?"

She stood and followed Cale. Pearl followed her. "How long have you had her?" When Maggie came to a stop, Pearl sat beside her as if waiting for a command of some sort. She wagged her tail so hard, her big body shook.

Maggie reached down to give the dog a scratch behind her long floppy ears. Pearl moaned in ecstasy seconds before she slid to the floor, her back leg scratching at nothing but air.

Cale opened the refrigerator and pulled out a pitcher of iced tea. "Since she was a pup. I was jogging on the beach one morning and suddenly there she was, running alongside me, dragging a string of barbed wire wrapped midway around her tail. After I took it off, she followed me home. No one bothered to claim her, not that I'd seriously consider allowing her to go back, given the shape the poor girl was in when she found me."

Not only did Maggie now understand the reason for the odd length of Pearl's bushy tail, but she'd discovered vitally important information regarding Cale. The man suffered from a hero complex. She didn't need to be Sigmund Freud to understand why Cale had become a paramedic. The injured pup revealed a lot about him and explained his rescuing *her* from an unknown fate.

There had to be more to the puzzle, of that she felt certain. For reasons she didn't understand, she couldn't help wondering about the *why* behind his good-hearted soul.

"Shake it, baby!"

Maggie stared at Cale, not quite certain she'd heard him right. "Pardon me?"

He pulled a pair of tall glasses from the cabinet nearest the sink. "Cool it, Gilda," he scolded on his way to the freezer for ice. "There's a lady in the house."

A wolf whistle came next. "Pretty mama. Yowza," was followed by a high-decibel screech.

This time Maggie had no trouble discerning the species or the location of the voice. She walked past Cale, through the efficiency kitchen into a cozy breakfast nook painted a soft white that matched the wicker table and chairs covered with bright print cushions. Potted palms and hanging ferns were scattered around the room, adding to the charm. A wind chime made entirely of seashells hung directly in front of the east window, complementing the tropical decor. She instantly liked this room. It'd be the perfect spot to...to what? Frustration filled her as the whisper-thin, indecipherable impression floated out of her grasp.

"Pucker up, doll."

Maggie turned toward the crude squawking. A large wrought-iron cage housing a predominately teal-colored parrot sat off to the side, away from the rays of streaming sunlight. "Hi there, Gilda," she said to the bird.

Cale entered the bright nook, a sheepish grin on his face. "She has a very unusual vocabulary for a girl," he said, wondering why on earth Maggie's interest in his pets gave him such a feeling of intense pleasure.

Maybe because most of the women he dated were either allergic, couldn't be bothered or just plain disliked animals, period.

Maggie grinned. The way her eyes sparkled when she glanced his way sent a shot of warmth through him. A very dangerous kind of warmth. The kind that jump-started fantasies—he remembered the color of Maggie's eyes when she was aroused and began to wonder if they'd become the color of the ocean if he kissed her pretty bow-shaped mouth.

"Where did you find her?" she asked, dragging him reluctantly out of his ocean-blue fantasy.

Gilda walked back and forth along her perch. "One of a kind. One of a kind."

"You most certainly are," she told the bird, her voice filled with a hint of laughter.

Gilda fluffed her brilliant feathers and squawked. The old girl knew a compliment when she heard one.

"Gilda's a long story," he hedged.

She gave him a sidelong look. "Sounds like an interesting one," she prompted.

Cale let out a sigh. "I was at a bachelor party for one of the guys at the station," he admitted sheepishly. "The owner of the place was looking for a home for Gilda, so I took her in."

A mischievous grin tugged her lips as she took the glass of iced tea he offered. "A bachelor party, huh?"

Gilda bobbed up and down to a tune all her own. "What a pair!"

Cale took a long drink of his own tea and looked away.

Maggie glanced at Gilda. "Careful," she scolded gently. "Uh, where exactly was this bachelor party?"

Cale rubbed the back of his neck, which had suddenly grown hot. "A place down the coast highway. You wouldn't know it."

"Shake it, baby."

"Based on Gilda's very unladylike choice of phrases, I think I have a pretty good idea."

"Ride 'em, cowgirl," Gilda belted, followed by a couple bars of the Lone Ranger's theme song.

Cale cleared his throat. "She was a lot worse a few months ago." Gilda still might be the linguistic equivalent of a dirty old man, but the swearing had begun to ebb...somewhat. Every now and then, however, she'd let loose with a string of curses so vile, she offended the neighbors.

"She sings, too," Cale told her. "Presley, Sinatra and Buddy Holly are her favorites." Maggie's soft gentle laughter, combined with the sensual curve of her lips had him thinking some very nonplatonic thoughts about his newest roommate.

"Any other critters I should be aware of?" she asked before taking a sip of her tea.

Cale led her away from Gilda before the bird started swearing. When Gilda had a live audience, anything was possible.

"Only Frankie and Johnnie," he said as he ushered Maggie back through the kitchen and into the living room. Pearl lay in the corner between the sofa and recliner on her bed, a large blue pillow stuffed with cedar wood chips.

"And they would be?"

"A pair of cats I got talked into adopting not long after I moved in here." He set his tea on the pine table and snagged the bag holding her things, preparing to give Maggie the nickel tour and show her to her room. The doctor had insisted she get plenty of rest over the next few days, and Cale had no intention of ignoring those orders, especially if it would help her with the return of her memory.

"They're all very lucky to have you." An odd expression filled her eyes. A hint of sorrow, naturally, but something deeper, more empathetic, reminding him that for the moment, he was the only person in the world who cared about what happened to Maggie With-No-Last-Name.

He knew what it was like to feel alone, sort of. Sure, he'd had his brothers and his father when his mother had died in the line of duty at a time when women firefighters were extremely rare. And then his aunt had stepped in when his father had simply given up on life after Joanna Perry had died. Although Cale hadn't been completely alone, he still had known a deep sense of longing for something familiar and comforting, something that remained elusive until eventually it faded with time. The perfume his mom used to wear when she was off duty, for instance, or the sweet, gentle sound of her voice as she read stories to her sons. Now he could barely remember the feel of his father's firm hand upon his shoulder or the deep rumble of his laughter.

His intent only to offer consolation, he dropped the bag at his feet before taking the glass of tea from Maggie's grasp. The moment he pulled her into his arms, she stiffened. A half second later, she let out a warm sigh and slid her arms around his waist. The heavy weight of her cast pressed into his side as he held her close. She smelled as warm and fresh as a summer day.

"You're not alone, Maggie," he whispered against her hair. "I'm here. I'm not going anywhere, and you're free to stay until you decide it's time for you to leave. Okay?"

He felt the slight nod of her head against his chest as he smoothed his hand down her back as if soothing a small child—except Maggie was no child. She was a full-grown woman with curves in all the right places. Curves he'd had the agonizing privilege of seeing when he'd walked in on her at the hospital. Curves he'd had the excruciating pleasure of touching as he'd helped her dress. Curves he was certain would haunt not only his dreams, but his waking hours, as well.

She pulled back to look up at him. Her eyes filled with moisture. "Cale," she whispered.

"Shh," he murmured, slipping his hand through her long cinnamon hair to cup the back of her neck in his palm. Comfort, that's all he was offering. It was all he had to offer.

The lie stuck in his suddenly dry throat as he slowly lowered his head, bringing their lips within inches of touching. Her dark sooty lashes fluttered closed as she lifted her lips to his. Kissing Maggie might not be his smartest move, but he'd started down this road and there was no way he could turn back now, not when she was such a willing participant.

His lips brushed hers just as the beeper clipped to his belt vibrated. For the space of a second he considered ignoring it, but he was on call, as were most of the guys at Trinity Station during off time. There was no such thing as being truly off duty in his line of work. Taking into account the time of day, he suspected the emergency was a multi-vehicle accident rather than a two-or three-alarm blaze.

"I'm sorry," he said as he released Maggie and reached for his beeper. The words "Six MVA on I-10," lit up the LCD screen, confirming his suspicions. It'd take him a minimum of fifteen, maybe twenty minutes, to be on the scene, but with six vehicles involved, the extra hands would be welcome regardless of when they arrived.

Reluctantly, he let her go. A sense of male satisfaction filled him at her obvious disappointment.

"I have to leave," he said, already feeling the rush of adrenaline creeping through his body as he anticipated the task ahead of him. "The guest room is downstairs. The lower level is pretty much under construction, but you'll be able to find it since it's the only room finished. Unfortunately, the working bathroom is upstairs at the moment. It's just down the hall."

He stepped around her and headed for the door.

"Is there anything I should do while you're gone?" she asked, stopping him as his hand settled on the doorknob. "Feed your pets, maybe?"

"Pearl likes to run along the beach about an hour

after she eats." He checked his watch, knowing he had to get going. "Give her a couple scoops of dry food if I'm not back by seven. Her food's in the tall cabinet next to the fridge. I can take her for a walk when I get home."

He didn't bother to say goodbye, just walked out the door without a backward glance. As he trotted down the steps and headed for his pickup, he was struck by the frightening thought that for the first time since following in his parents' professional footsteps, his focus was on something other than just doing his job; it was on the woman who'd be waiting for him at the end of the day.

# 4

*THEY GOT lucky this time.*

Cale stepped beneath the hot, stinging spray of the locker-room shower. A six-car pileup during rush hour on any of Los Angeles's many freeways could have easily meant several injuries and possible fatalities. The two most serious patients had already been removed by another team of paramedics by the time Cale and Brady had arrived at the scene.

Although still in serious condition, the driver of the second vehicle, which had been sandwiched between two cars, had ended up with nothing more life-threatening than a tib/fib fracture. From what Cale had gleaned from the highway patrolmen at the scene, the driver in car number two hadn't even had a chance to apply the brakes before slamming into the lead vehicle, which had stalled in the fast lane, courtesy of a bad fuel pump.

The driver of the third car was a little luckier and only suffered a broken arm along with a couple of bruised ribs. The rest of the injured, including the driver of the lead vehicle, had been treated at the scene for contusions and lacerations before being transported to the UCLA Medical Center for further treatment or observation.

Personal experience and six years on the job told Cale the call could've been a whole lot worse. There'd be no rustling up the stress team to debrief the crews who'd worked the scene. No one had died. No one had been injured beyond recognition. The crew from Trinity Station could all go home and feel good about their jobs today.

A slow smile tugged Cale's lips as he plucked the soap from the holder and started scrubbing the sweat and grime from his body. *Home.* Home, where a beautiful, intriguing woman waited for him. A woman with a sassy glint in her eye that had him nearly kissing her despite the hint of uncertainty and confusion banked there as well. The last thing he wanted to do was add to Maggie's already confused state, but had he ever been tempted! So tempted the thought of kissing her hadn't felt all that inappropriate, which probably should have bothered him on some level, except it didn't. There were a thousand reasons for keeping his hands to himself, yet that didn't stop him from *wanting*, and very nearly following through on the desire to taste her sweet, bow-shaped mouth. Those thousands of reasons even failed to quell the urgent need to trace his fingers over the gentle curve of her hip, to feel the small of her back against his hands, to urge their bodies closer together and allow nature, and his lust, to follow their natural courses.

The woman had temptation written all over her body, and that equaled trouble in Cale's mind. But whoever said trouble was a bad thing obviously had never had a captivating woman sharing his living space.

"Hey, save some hot water for the rest of us."

The bar of soap slipped from Cale's fingers as he snapped his head around to find his eldest brother, Ben, standing in the shower area, a white cotton towel slung around his hips. He'd been part of the six-man engine crew called to the scene. It'd only be a matter of minutes before the rest of the crew filed into the locker room.

Cale offered his brother a sheepish grin. "Sorry. I was thinking."

Ben's left eyebrow rose, his expression filled with blatant curiosity. Well, as far as Cale was concerned, big brother could just remain in the dark on this one. Cale had no intention of sharing the status of his current living arrangements with either one of his brothers...yet. He knew he would eventually, but it'd be nice to have some privacy for a change, even if only for a brief period of time.

Although he had no reason to feel guilty, he sure as hell did, considering how defensive he'd sounded at being caught daydreaming. Still, it wasn't as if he'd been in the middle of some erotic fantasy casting his own personal mystery woman in the leading role.

Okay, so he'd been close. Shoot him.

Ben said nothing as he stepped into the vacant stall next to Cale's, slapped his towel over the bluish marble half wall and turned on the steaming spray. Although the eldest Perry brother tended to be the more silent of the three, when it came to his family, the still-water routine ended and became a steadily flowing river of overprotectiveness. Ben still believed it was his right to share his opinion on any situation, something Cale and Drew both dreaded.

With anyone outside the family, Ben pretty much kept to himself. Come to think of it, Cale had a hard time remembering the last time Ben had even bothered to join the guys at the Ivory Turtle for a beer or to attend any of the backyard barbecues one of the crew might have hosted. He wasn't what Cale would call aloof, because Ben did have a good rapport with everyone at Trinity Station. He had a good sense of humor, too, and could always be counted on being included in any of the practical jokes they were all so fond of playing on one another.

Cale knew Ben had his reasons for being pretty much a loner. When their mother had died, Cale had been eight years old and Drew six, and Ben had stepped up and assumed as much of a parental role as a ten-year-old boy could handle. All of their lives had become drastically altered when they'd lost their mom, but in Cale's opinion, Ben had suffered the deepest effects of their loss. Not only had he shouldered the responsibility of his younger brothers, Ben had dealt with their broken-hearted old man, and had done his best to shield Cale and Drew from the rapid decline of Alex Perry.

When their father had passed away less than two years later, the boys had gone to live with their dad's sister, Deborah Perry. Instead of letting their aunt step in and take over as parent in their lives, Ben clung to his assumed role as the "man of the house." As a result, he'd sacrificed more than any young man should have been expected to in order to keep the three of them together. There'd been plenty of times Cale and Drew had resented Ben's interference in their lives, but Cale wasn't stupid enough to believe he hadn't become the man he was today in part due to his brother's influence. He not only loved his brother, but he respected him, even when Ben did butt in where Cale or Drew felt he shouldn't.

Ben broke the silence. "Good job today."

"Easy run."

"Could've been a lot worse."

"Yeah. Could've been." Cale dipped his head beneath the spray. Something was on Ben's mind. He knew his brother's moods, and small talk more often than not meant a lead-in to some other topic, one that usually had Ben pumping him for information or ready to spout some well-meaning lecture.

Cale obviously couldn't stay under the spray forever, so he shut off the water and reached for his towel, planning a quick escape instead.

Ben wouldn't have it. "Drew tells me Tilly's seen your truck in the parking lot of the hospital nearly every night this past week."

Damn. Cale had been so sure by using the main parking lot he'd avoid being seen. Figures it would be Tilly to bust him and rat him out to Drew.

Tilly Jensen, their next-door neighbor once they'd moved in with Debbie, was the closest thing the Perry boys had to a sister. To this day, Tilly and Drew were as close as twins. Tilly had lost her mother at a young age, too, and lived alone with her father. Cale's aunt had filled a void in all of their lives.

So much for anonymity, he thought. He considered

evading the comment, but he knew from experience that would only heighten Ben's curiosity, along with his protective nature. Cale didn't want or need big brother to start snooping around, but he couldn't falsely accuse Drew or Tilly of being liars, either.

Cale dried off, anxious to avoid interrogation. "I've been visiting a friend," he offered, hoping to put an end to this conversation as quickly as possible.

"Yeah? Which one?"

He wasn't fooled by Ben's nonchalance. He knew a bloodhound when he saw one. "Someone you haven't met." He tied the towel around his waist. "What's with all the questions?"

"Why are you evading my questions?"

"Oh, I don't know. Ever hear of a little thing called privacy?"

Before Ben could comment further, Cale turned and headed toward his locker just as Brady and more of the guys from the engine crew began to file into the room. Finally, a reprieve...that lasted all of two minutes.

Ben reappeared and opened his locker, which was only two down from Cale's. "I can find out, you know. Tilly would tell me if I asked her for specifics."

Cale let out an exasperated huff of breath. "I just can't win, can I?"

Ben grinned, something he didn't do nearly often enough.

"Fine," Cale complained. "Her name is Maggie. Satisfied?"

Brady chuckled as he started removing his gear. "So that explains the goofball look."

Cale frowned at his partner. "Goofball? Now wait just a minute..."

"I had a feeling it was a woman," Ben said.

"It's *not* a woman. Not the way you're thinking." That wasn't a total lie. Was it?

Ivan "Fitz" Fitzpatrick slung his hand over the top of the door to his own locker. "Is she young?"

Cale shrugged. Great. Now the entire house would know about Maggie. "Around twenty-eight or so," he guessed. "Maybe a little younger."

"I bet she's pretty," Noah Harding, the main driver of the engine crew, added.

Cale's frown deepened. "Yeah, so?"

"What's her problem?" Tom "Scorch" Mc-Donough called from the other side of the row of lockers.

Cale really hated that his personal life was no longer personal and shot a glare at his brother for opening this line of questioning. "What does that have to do with anything?" Cale shouted to Scorch.

The fellow paramedic walked around the row of lockers. "Young, pretty and in need of a knight in shining armor. Classic Cale Perry." Scorch nodded toward the door. "Right, Drew?"

"I could hear you guys all the way downstairs in the day room," Drew said. "What's up?"

Hank Martinez, another member of the engine crew, dropped onto the wooden bench in front of his locker. "Cale's found himself another damsel in distress."

Drew grinned and, as usual, Cale was struck by old memories of his mom. There was something about the way his little brother's mouth tipped upward, just like Mom's had when she'd been amused.

"Is that so?" Drew crossed his arms over his chest and leaned against the doorjamb. "Who is she?"

Ben spoke up. "The name Maggie ring any bells?"

"Maggie?" Brady asked, his dark eyebrows tugging downward. "You mean the broad from the paint warehouse?"

Cale tucked his shirt into his jeans, his frown deepening farther as he glared at Brady. "She's not a 'broad.'"

Fitz laughed good-naturedly while he nudged Chance Mitchell with his elbow. "Defensive, ain't he?"

"Yeah, Cale," Chance added. "Why are you getting your boxers in a twist?"

"He must be involved with her," Drew said with an all-knowing nod of his head.

Cale scowled at the guys, his younger brother in particular. As if Drew should talk. He was the one with the revolving bedroom door, not Cale. "I'm not *involved* with anyone."

"Except the broad from the paint-warehouse fire," Brady clarified.

"The redhead?" Noah let out a low whistle. "Man, she's a looker."

The guys might be simply giving him a good old-fashioned hard time, something they all did regularly because it helped them blow off some steam, but Cale sure as hell didn't want them referring to Maggie as a "broad" or even a "looker." He wasn't about to question the whys behind it, either. That would mean admitting he had feelings he wasn't willing to say existed. She was, after all, a total stranger.

Instead, he shifted his attention to Drew. As an arson inspector, Drew could have answers to questions that might help her rediscover her identity. "Has there been any word on the cause of the fire at the Harrison Paint and Wallpaper warehouse yet?" he asked Drew.

His brother pushed off the wall and walked toward Cale. "It wasn't my scene. I could find out, though. Why?"

"Because Maggie doesn't know who she is. I was hoping maybe someone—an employee, the owner, anyone—might know who she is and why she was in the warehouse."

The guys that hadn't made it into the showers yet stopped cold and stared at Cale. *Oh, great, here we go.*

"What did you say?" Drew questioned.

The look on Ben's face wasn't filled with half of the surprise that was on Drew's. In fact, Ben appeared more resigned, as if he'd expected something like this.

"Cale, what have you done this time?" Drew asked him.

"Nothing!" he said defensively. "I'm just trying to help her, that's all. Besides, it's only temporary." Too late, he realized his mistake.

"What do you mean 'temporary'?" Ben asked. "She's living with you, isn't she?"

Brady let out a sigh. "Here we go again."

"What do you guys know?" Cale groused none too politely.

"You," his brothers, Scorch and Brady all said in unison.

Cale ignored the concern in Ben's eyes. Instead, he focused on the rabble-rousers and crossed his arms over his chest. "And your point is...?"

"Gracie Kennedy," Drew supplied.

Chance nodded in agreement. "Oh, yeah. A perfect example."

"She needed my help," Cale argued, unwilling to publicly admit he'd allowed himself to be conned...although he hadn't minded at the time. Gracie had a body made for sin and had been damned generous in sharing it with him.

Scorch shoved a hand through his flame-red hair, but the permanent case of bed-head refused to be tamed by something as innocuous as his freckled fingers. "She needed you to help move her, what? Three, four times?" he reminded them.

Cale sat on the bench to slip his feet into his tennis shoes and grinned. "Ever help a woman set up a bed?" When Scorch gave him a blank stare, he added, "They like to try them out."

"What about Paulette Johnson?" Chance asked.

"I remember her," Brady added and cringed dramatically. "A real cling-on."

Cale remembered her, too. Big green eyes, lethal curves and pouty red lips.

He glanced up at his partner. "Okay, so she was a little insecure."

Brady laughed. "A little? You had to turn off your cell phone whenever we were on a call because she wouldn't leave you alone." He looked at Ben and

Scorch. "Did you know she even bought a police scanner so she could keep tabs on Cale?"

"That's not needy," Scorch said. "That's creepy."

"Stalker material," Chance added.

Cale tied his shoes. "She wasn't all that bad," he muttered, but deep in his gut, he couldn't really disagree. Paulette *had* become a little too possessive...something a restraining order had eventually cured.

"Remember Tracy Newton?" Brady asked the guys.

"Wasn't she the one who tried to sweet-talk Cale into marrying her?" Drew asked.

Scorch laughed. "No, that was Shelby Monroe. Tracy buffaloed him into house-sitting for her while she went to Palm Springs—with some other guy."

He couldn't argue since Tracy had definitely played him for a fool.

Cale sighed. It wasn't that all women took advantage of him. And while he did admit on the surface it appeared he had a penchant for women with problems, not every woman in his life held the title of temporary damsel in distress. Well, maybe most of them, but definitely not *all* of them.

Cale stood and closed his locker. "It's not what you're thinking. This time it's different."

That statement brought gales of laughter from the crew of Trinity Station.

"They're all different," Drew reminded him.

Cale had had enough abuse for one night. "I'm outta here. You guys can dissect Ben's love life. Oh, wait," he said with a snap of his fingers and shot his brother a look. "Ben doesn't have a love life. Well, try picking on Scorch. I hear he's all hot and bothered over some nurse."

Scorch sputtered in response, sent a nervous glance in Drew's direction, then blushed a shade of crimson even brighter than his hair, if that was possible.

To Drew, Cale quietly murmured, "See what you can find out about the paint warehouse for me, okay?"

Drew slapped his hand on Cale's shoulder. "Sure thing, brother. I'll stop by in the morning."

"Why doesn't that surprise me? Ben coming, too?" Now that his brothers knew about Maggie, only an act of God would keep them from satisfying their curiosity.

Drew's smile widened. "Did you for a minute think we wouldn't?"

Cale let out a sigh, resigning himself to the fact he'd never have a personal life that didn't include his brothers' interference in one form or another. "No," he said as he headed for the door. "But a guy can hope, can't he?"

# 5

*SHE WAS going to be late if she didn't hurry. Juggling her black Italian baguette purse and the letter-sized box secured with a scarlet ribbon while she shrugged into her trench coat, she managed to tap the button on her answering machine. A quick brush at a piece of lint on her sleeve, and she reached for the door. One useless pull, and nothing happened. The darned thing was stuck again.*

*She swore softly. Despite being rushed, she smiled briefly, recalling a woman's gently scolding voice. "You might step in it, dear, but a lady should never say it."*

*Giving the base of the door a swift kick with the toe of her overpriced black calfskin flats, she tugged again. Still no luck. The doorman was holding a cab for her, her bags were already loaded. The meter was ticking, and not just in the cabbie's favor. She needed to drop off the package, and if she didn't escape her apartment in the next five seconds, she might even miss her flight.*

*Whacking the door once more with her foot, she yanked hard, then stumbled when the door swung wide, knocking her off balance. She made a note to remind the building superintendent about the warped door. Now that summer had officially arrived, turning the climate from hot to hotter, as well as unbearably humid almost overnight, the sticking door would only get worse. Since she'd be out of town for at least a month, it'd be the perfect time for him to fix the problem.*

*With one last look around her cozy apartment while running though her list to make sure the appliances were unplugged and the gas turned off on the stove, she slipped over the threshold. As she turned to secure the locks, a large male hand grabbed hold of her shoulder...*

SOMEWHERE, in that place between sleep and wakefulness, Maggie carefully eased her body slightly to the left and readjusted her cast on the throw pillow beside her. She heard the soft snore of Pearl resting on the floor next to the sofa. Maggie opened her eyes briefly and realized that night had fallen. Frankie or Johnny, she still didn't know which was which, lay curled next to her hip, while her counterpart bathed herself on the back of the sofa. That must've been what Maggie had felt—Johnny or Frankie alighting on the perch above her because, other than Cale's pets, she was definitely alone.

Strange, she thought. For the first time since she'd awoken in the hospital a little over a week ago, she felt safe and oddly secure. She breathed in, then tugged the homemade afghan higher over her chest, closed her eyes and waited for sleep to reclaim her.

*MAGGIE KEPT her back to the wall and crouched low, expertly maintaining her balance so as not to set off the intricate laser alarm system protecting the floor safe. The safe, which she believed held the blueprints of the Louvre's storage area where the priceless artifacts were kept, was her primary target. She could care less about the forty-carat dia-*

mond-cut ruby that supposedly had belonged to Nefertiti, although there had been a time in Maggie's career when the gem would have been her sole purpose. She'd been damned good at her job...once.

Part of her missed those days, but she had to admit her life served a higher purpose now, even if the legitimate job market for someone in her line of work was slim to none. The competitiveness still stimulated her, and there weren't many people on the planet with the ability to do what she did. It was in her blood. She was one of the best cat burglars, certainly, but there was only one person she would openly admit was better. Fortunately, their paths hadn't crossed in about two years. In fact, she fully expected to find him in the area considering the value of the rare manuscript illuminations that had arrived at the museum less than three months ago.

Several attempts had already been made against the jewels, but Nefertiti's ruby remained untouched, and Maggie had no plans to change that status.

She'd studied the laser pattern for weeks. Obtaining the security details of the Louvre had been a walk in the park. A little up-close-and-personal time with the head of security, snatching the plans then having them reproduced and returning the originals before anyone had been the wiser, had been a ridiculously simple task. Too easy, which always made her err on the side of caution.

She pulled an aerosol can filled with water from the slim backpack holding her tools and prepared to spray the area to obtain a clear visual of the lattice pattern surrounding the floor safe.

Her hand stilled. She heard her name, a soft, gentle whis-

*per that could only be her imagination. No. That wasn't right. Someone had actually called her name.*

*Impossible. Wasn't it? No one knew she was in Paris. She hadn't seen him in nearly two years, not since she'd turned. Still, she'd easily wager her numbered Swiss account she'd just heard his voice.*

*She remained still, listening. Only the gentle hum of the air-conditioning met her ears. That, and the rapid cadence of her own heartbeat.*

*"Maggie?"*

*Her palms started to sweat. He never called her Maggie. To him she was always Margaret Elizabeth.*

*She lost her grip on the aerosol can. As if watching herself from above, she saw the can slip from her fingers. She stared, stunned, as it floated onto the marble floor where it clattered and rolled toward the laser beams. Any second now, the high-tech system would send an alert that security had been breached.*

*She parlayed her attention between the shadows and the can. Had she heard something else? No, a movement had caught her attention.*

*She peered deeper into the shadows. There he stood. She couldn't see his face clearly, yet she knew it was him.*

*The can rolled to a stop a hairbreadth away from setting off the alarm.*

*He stepped forward ever so slightly into the pale, thin ray of moonlight and extended his hand. Dangling from his fingertips was a red silk handkerchief with an embroidered V.*

"MAGGIE?"

Maggie struggled to escape the voice threatening to

pull her out of the dream. The firm grip on her shoulder and the gentle hand shaking her had her opening her eyes.

Soft light illuminated the room, but this time she found no comfort, none of the sense of well-being she'd experienced earlier. Still haunted from the disturbing images running through her mind, she shivered.

My God, who was she? Worse, *what* was she? Some kind of thief? That much was unfortunately obvious. But if she was indeed a thief, wouldn't she have been fingerprinted at least once in her…career, for lack of a better word? And if she had been printed, why hadn't anything shown up when the locals tried to I.D. her? Surely they would've accessed the FBI's extensive computer system.

Nothing added up, unless she was such a good crook she'd just never been caught. Adding to her confusion was the first segment of her dream. She'd been in a hurry. She'd had an apartment, which she was pretty certain had been located in a large metropolitan area if she took into account the doorman and the cab that had been waiting for her. It had been as if she were a "normal" person, not a criminal. Unless the package she'd been carrying had been the booty from a recent job, but for reasons she had little hope of explaining at this point, she didn't believe that to be the case.

"Maggie? Are you all right?"

No, she wasn't all right. She was scared, confused and about eighty percent certain she'd operated on the wrong side of the law.

"I was dreaming," she said evasively. Despite being radically spooked, she couldn't help the feeling of awe. For the first time since the explosion, instead of wisps of memory every now and then, she recalled with distinct clarity the details provided by her subconscious...even if she didn't like what she'd just learned.

She looked up at Cale and stared, mesmerized by his sexier-than-sin blue eyes. Though still emotionally rattled by the dream, she almost sighed at the mere sight of him. Certainly not because he loomed over her, trapping her between his large, warm body and the buttery soft leather sofa as he gently shook her awake.

No, that couldn't be it.

She was merely relieved not to be alone after learning she could very well be nothing more than a common thief. Could that have been the reason she'd been alone in the paint warehouse? Had she been after something? But what?

The increased pounding of her heart had absolutely nothing to do with the unexpected sharp tug of desire suddenly demanding attention and everything to do with a disturbing revelation about her possibly nefarious identity.

At least that's what she wanted to believe. And maybe, just maybe, she was somewhere in the vicinity of the truth.

"I was dreaming," she repeated. She didn't bother to push herself up into a sitting position. In fact, as she lay back against the throw pillow, the sudden urge to reach up with her good hand and pull his head down to hers, to slip her mouth over his and lose herself in what she suspected would be a bone-melting kiss, overwhelmed her nearly as much as the strange, disjointed dream had spooked her.

She attempted to convince herself she merely sought comfort, in any form, a thought that died a quick death thanks to the increasing need to feel Cale's lips against hers, to feel his hands gliding hungrily over her body. Maybe all she really wanted was to touch something real, not a misty haunting image.

Cale nudged her hip as he shifted his position on the sofa beside her. "What kind of dream?"

His tone might have been absolutely nonsexual, but that didn't quell the desire to be near him.

"I have an apartment somewhere." She opted to keep what could very well be her profession, along with her ill-timed runaway fantasies, to herself for the time being. "Or I did have one. I can't say for sure."

"You remembered something."

She nodded and tried not to wince at the hope tingeing his voice.

The smile that eased across his mouth made her heart stop. Her life, or what was left of it, was nothing but a jumbled mess and here she was lying beside a handsome, virile man, completely turned on because he had a killer smile that made her feel all warm and fuzzy inside. What kind of lunatic was she?

"Then that's good news." His smile widened. "Do you remember anything else?"

She looked away, her gaze zeroing in on his strong hands, his long fingers resting on the dark denim covering his thighs. Rock-hard thighs, too, she thought, remembering the feel of them cushioning her head when she'd been treated following the warehouse explosion.

Foolishly, she didn't stop there, but allowed her gaze to wander lasciviously.

Breathing suddenly became a concentrated effort as a tidal wave of pure, unadulterated lust crashed into her. Heat uncurled through her body as she devoured the sight of his jeans clinging to his body, leaving no doubt in her mind whatsoever that he was having the same ridiculous and dangerous thoughts as her. Gracious, they hadn't even touched, or kissed for that matter.

*Oh, this is not a good sign.*

*Yeah, but all the signs say he'll be really good.*

That thought truly shocked her, which only managed to add to her surprise and confusion. Was she a prude? Or was it really like her to be so brazen? Considering that she might be a crook, she couldn't say whether her train of thought was the status quo or some freaky side trip down the who-am-I? highway. She supposed it didn't really matter. So long as she refused to act out these wicked and oh-so-lovely fantasies she'd started having, then she had nothing to worry about.

She hoped.

Boy, did she ever have her doubts on *that* score. Her purgatory points were mounting up against her, in triplicate.

"Maggie?" He sounded concerned.

He should, considering where her mind continued to wander.

She reluctantly dragged her gaze away from forbidden territory. "I think I'd like to get up now."

He didn't move. His hip resting against hers reminded her exactly how close they were. Not that she needed a reminder. Her racing pulse was doing a fine job.

"Are you sure everything is all right?"

She pulled in a deep breath and with it, Cale's scent, a combination of spice and soap and male warmth. "Fine. I could just use a little air is all." Not exactly a lie, because she not only needed air to clear her mind and start putting all her conflicting emotions and thoughts into some sort of discernable order, but she desperately needed space from Cale. If she didn't distance herself soon, she'd do something really stupid, like give into that bone-melting kiss fantasy.

"Pearl hasn't been for her evening walk yet, anyway," she added lamely.

He looked at her steadily for a minute, but didn't say a word, just stood and extended his hand to assist her from the sofa. She avoided his gaze—and his hand—swinging her feet to the floor and standing on her own. Maggie knew she was acting strangely, but with any luck, he wouldn't think her any more bizarre than usual.

Besides, how normal could a woman without a memory behave anyway?

"You sure everything is okay?" he pressed, his

voice laced with concern, which only increased her already guilty conscience.

So much for him not noticing her behavior. "I'm fine." She chanced a quick look in his direction. His dark eyebrows pulled together slightly, his expression telling her loud and clear he wasn't swallowing the line she'd tried to feed him. "Just a little confused," she added with a smile. She aimed for bright but ended up with brittle instead.

Cále shrugged. "I guess you'll tell me when you're ready." He left the room only to return less than a minute later with a lightweight jacket for her and a black leather lead for Pearl.

How was it possible that someone who didn't know her, could know her so well? And why did she feel so badly for not being perfectly honest with him? That was hardly a characteristic common to a person who operated on the wrong side of the legal system.

Since quick answers evaded her, she slipped into the jacket and tried on what she hoped was a smile this time rather than a grimace as she rolled back the sleeves. The scent of Cale surrounded her, but she used every ounce of her swiftly decreasing willpower not to bury her face in the lightweight fabric and let her imagination run wild.

She followed Cale and Pearl out the front door, tugged the jacket tighter around her and breathed in anyway.

CALE TURNED Pearl loose to let her run along the shoreline once they reached the beach. Maggie walked silently alongside him, a worried frown marring her delicate features. His intuition that she was keeping something from him mounted. Certainly, if she'd had some clue that could lead them to her identity, she'd share it with him.

Wouldn't she?

Not only did he dislike the fact that her behavior had started raising doubts in him, but the idea that she'd keep something important from him, or that she felt she *couldn't* share with him whatever glimpse of her past she'd had, said a lot about the level of trust between them. And that bothered him. Up until now, she'd trusted him. What had changed in the few hours he'd been away?

She was with him so he could help her. How did she expect him to do so if she wouldn't let him in and continued to keep things to herself? Maybe, he thought as he walked toward a large piece of driftwood, she just needed time to come to terms with whatever she'd recently discovered before talking it over with him.

Pearl trotted along the edge of the water beneath the moonlight before sprinting toward her favorite sand dune. Cale indicated the driftwood and waited for Maggie to sit before he joined her.

"You learned something, didn't you?" So much for giving her time to think about whatever information she'd gleaned from her dream, he thought.

She let out a soft sigh and glanced at him. Her troubled gaze locked with his, and his heart squeezed ever so slightly. He tried to ignore the sensation.

"I did," she finally admitted.

He leaned forward to rest his elbows on his knees,

letting his hands dangle between his thighs. The end of Pearl's lead teased the ground between his sneakers as he traced a lazy pattern in the sand. "And?"

"I just don't know if the dream was real or not, but I heard a woman's voice that sounded familiar."

The doctors had said her memory would eventually return, but no one had said a word about it coming back to her in her sleep. Still, a lead was a lead, and he wasn't about to discount any piece of information that could very well help Maggie regain her identity.

"Let's assume for the moment it was real." He looked over at her, and his heart twisted again at the worry encompassing her delicate features. He compounded his mistake by allowing his gaze to dip to her mouth, tight with worry. The desire to soften those lips with his own hit him hard in the gut. "Did you see the woman?" he asked, hoping to draw his concentration back to the issues at hand.

Maggie slowly shook her head. "No, I just *heard* her. You know when you remember something that someone once said to you? It was like that."

He understood more than she knew, having experienced the same sensation many times over the years since the death of his parents.

"You know who was speaking?"

She let out another sigh. "No."

"Where were you when you heard the voice? What were you doing?"

"In my apartment. At least I *think* it was my apartment. I mean, it *felt* like it was mine. I was in a hurry and the front door was stuck, so I kicked it and swore. That's when I heard the woman's voice."

She looked away again, and Cale had the distinct impression she was still withholding some information. He could either dwell on what she wasn't telling him, or focus on what she had revealed in an effort to help her discover more about herself. While the former interested him more, he struggled to focus on the latter.

"Tell me about your apartment?" he asked. "Do you know where it was located? Could you see what was inside?"

"Inside?"

"A bookshelf, a stereo, CDs, that fragile stuff women like to collect? What about paintings or posters? What kind of furniture did it have? Can you remember anything distinct?"

He watched as she furrowed her brow, and took on a faraway look. Her frown deepened farther until she finally shook her head. "No, nothing." Frustration lined her voice.

"Why don't you try closing your eyes," he suggested gently. "See if you can recall the smallest detail."

He knew he wasn't supposed to pressure her to remember, but whether it was for his own benefit or hers, he couldn't say. Had it become a simple matter of trust, or was there some other motivation at work he had yet to determine?

Before he could draw a conclusion to his own questions, she sighed and did as he asked. A soft breeze ruffled her cinnamon hair, tossing a few strands across her face. She pushed them away, but kept her eyes closed.

In the distance, a car backfired. Before he could draw his next breath, Maggie moved. She took hold of his arm in an iron-tight grip with her good hand while her cast clunked against the back of his neck. Next thing he knew, he was lying facedown in the sand with her body draped over his, both of them protected by the shadow of the huge piece of driftwood.

"What the—"

"Quiet," she whispered harshly.

She rose up slightly, her hips pressing seductively against his backside. He attempted to crane his neck so he could see what she was doing, but her cast slammed into the back of his head again, shoving his face into the sand. Vainly, he struggled to decipher her erratic behavior, but the feel of her curves and the way they pressed against his back, the way his body responded with rapt attention, clouded his better judgment. The battle had been lost before it even began.

"Stay down," she ordered, her voice firm and strangely controlled.

He pulled his arm out from beneath him and wiped the sand from his face. "Uh, Maggie?"

"Shh," she whispered in a harsh, take-no-prisoners tone.

Her cast landed on the back of his head again, but he quickly rolled until he had her pinned beneath him. Her breathing was ragged, and her breasts brushed against his chest creating one hell of a distraction.

"No," she said. "It might not be safe yet."

"What's going on, Maggie?"

"Someone just took a shot at us. Now stay down before you get us both killed."

## 6

IF SHE weren't so damned serious, he would have burst out laughing. "Maggie, a car backfired. Nothing more."

Holding her wrist and cast above her head with his hands, he looked down into her eyes. He expected fear. Instead, he discovered something else entirely that sent his heart ricocheting behind his ribs—desire.

Her gaze dipped to his mouth. "Are you absolutely certain?"

Her soft, loverlike voice stroked his already heightened awareness, leaving him to struggle like the devil to concentrate on her strange behavior rather than the way his hips were practically locked against hers.

This was one battle he knew he had little chance of winning.

"Positive," he told her.

She relaxed, her body melting beneath his. He should let her go to save them both from making a monumental mistake. Except there was no denying he wanted her, and the way her lips parted and her eyes searched his face left little doubt in his mind that her thoughts had taken the same treacherous path as his own.

He didn't move so much as an inch. There'd be

time for explanations later. All his befuddled, lust-controlled mind had the capacity of analyzing was how perfect her body felt against his, how soft her lips would feel, how sweet she'd taste when...

He never had a chance to finish the thought. Lowering his head, he brushed his mouth over hers in a light, tentative kiss. Her sharp intake of breath, followed by a wispy little moan of pleasure, let him know they were thinking alike.

She took the initiative and deepened their kiss. Her luscious curves lifted urgently against him as her body arched into his. Any second thoughts he might have harbored given the chance, evaporated into thin air.

He welcomed her teasing, coaxing tongue to mate with his until his ears buzzed and his body hummed. His heart pounded rapidly in his chest as he lost himself in the taste of her, in her intoxicating scent, a unique, scrumptious blend of woman and misty sea breeze.

Oh, man, was he ever in trouble. Not only did he have a warm and willing woman in his arms, but the temperature of his blood rose to new levels that had his libido taking off like a rocket.

She strained against his light grip so he released her, only to smooth his hands along her body, marveling at every gentle dip and swell. She slipped her leg around his calf, holding him captive against her.

Maggie rocked her hips against his, and he nearly went into cardiac arrest. Her slender fingers boldly explored his shoulders, then ran enticingly from back to buttocks where she urged him tighter against her.

His erection strained against the confining denim to the point of pleasurable pain. Losing control wasn't something he relished, but he was close to being past the point of caring. If he didn't have her soon, all of her, he'd go crazy.

Pearl's cold wet nose nudged hard at the side of his neck.

He gently tried to push the dog away, only to receive a low "woof" next to his ear. When Pearl wanted his attention, she certainly knew how to get it.

Maggie giggled against his mouth.

He made a noise that sounded a whole lot like a growl of frustration, then deepened the kiss again, intending to ignore Pearl for a few more minutes and draw Maggie back into the moment.

He trailed his mouth along the tender flesh just below her ear. She rocked against him again and issued another of her soft, gentle sighs that had his already dangerously high testosterone level simmering.

Pearl, on the other hand, refused to be ignored. The big dog groaned and laid her bulky head on his back before letting out a sigh gusty enough to ruffle the hair on the back of his head.

A guy just couldn't win. With his own reluctant sigh, he lifted his head and looked over his shoulder at the dog. "What?"

Pearl immediately sat. Her stubby tail swished in the sand and her teeth practically glowed in the moonlight when she showed him her doggie smile. A piece of driftwood lay between her paws.

"It's not playtime," he said. Well, maybe it was, but not the kind Pearl wanted.

"Cale?"

He looked down at Maggie, at the desire turning her eyes a deep shade of turquoise, then over at Pearl, tail still wagging, tongue lolling out the side of her mouth as she waited expectantly for him to pick up the stick and throw it for her.

With a final groan of frustration, he eased himself away from Maggie. His decision wasn't based entirely on Pearl's need for her nightly playtime ritual, but more on his own need to regain control. If it hadn't been for Pearl, he honestly couldn't say how far he'd have gone, or exactly how far Maggie would have allowed them to travel down the enticing path toward mutual gratification.

Whether that was a good thing or not, he couldn't say for certain. He was supposed to be helping Maggie, not confusing her even more by his inability to keep his hands, or his lips, to himself.

As much as he hated the pleasure to end, he reluctantly stood and held out his hand for Maggie. She looked at him, and he instantly felt regret. Confusion colored her eyes now, along with the remnants of desire.

Damn.

He helped her up, then stooped to pick up the stick and toss it for Pearl to retrieve.

"Should I apologize?" he asked.

Maggie remained silent as she brushed the sand from her jeans with her good hand. When she glanced up at him, a hint of a smile curved her mouth. "Not unless you're sorry you kissed me."

Pearl brought back the piece of driftwood and dropped it at his feet. He chucked the stick again.

He reached for Maggie and pulled her to his side before he smoothed the back of his hand gently down her smooth-as-satin cheek. "I'm not sorry I kissed you," he told her softly.

Her smile turned shy. "I'm glad."

For the next ten minutes, there was silence between them while he played fetch with Pearl. It wasn't an awkward kind of silence, either, he mused. There was no frantic search for some inane topic for discussion. This was quiet, a companionable silence, the kind he thought he remembered his parents had often shared.

His thoughts reaffirmed his earlier assessment. Maggie was trouble with a capital *T,* especially if she had him thinking in terms of how compatible they were together. He'd been with his fair share of women, but he honestly couldn't remember the last time a simple kiss had made him lose his sense of time and place. He'd always been aware of his surroundings, but this time, it'd been different. The thought should've spooked him rather than make him smile like a…goofball?

Far from overjoyed with his train of thought, he turned to face Maggie, hoping to find an answer for a question he had earlier. "Do you want to explain what happened before…before we were distracted," he finished sheepishly.

The smile left her face, and she bit her lower lip again. "An overreaction?"

Now there was an understatement if he'd ever heard one. But that didn't explain how Maggie knew the sound of a gunshot, or even why she'd mistakenly believed someone would be shooting at her.

He gave her a sidelong glance. "You think?"

She shrugged. The wind gusted and whipped her spicy hair into even more disarray. She turned away from the wind and vainly attempted to finger-comb the strands into a semblance of order. "Maybe we should head back. I think I need to place a call to Detective Villanueva."

He frowned. "What on earth for? No one was shooting at you, Maggie. It was just a car backfiring."

She cleared her throat and unwaveringly held his gaze. "Because, Cale. I'm pretty sure there's a really good chance that I'm a criminal."

If Cale laughed one more time, she just might haul off and slug him one in the arm. Hard, too. Really, *really* hard.

She found absolutely no humor in the knowledge she might be a hardened criminal. In fact, now that she thought about it, she was downright appalled. Maybe the knock on her head wasn't such a bad thing after all, especially if it had made her realize she was a less-than-stellar member of society. Perhaps she'd just been handed the opportunity for redemption.

No doubt about it, her emotions were in a messy tangle. Not only was she disgusted by her possible profession, she was equally astounded at her little brazen act on the beach with Cale. It hadn't been as if she hadn't enjoyed every sensual second of that kiss.

No, what really had her confusion mounting faster than the national debt was the simple fact that she hadn't wanted it to end. Right there in front of Mother Nature and all her minions, she'd have been an extremely willing participant in the horizontal mambo.

And that wasn't the worst of it, either. She might have been an extremely willing participant, but in the past few days, her actions with Cale had felt absolutely, one-hundred-percent right. Not sure if she believed in happily ever afters did absolutely nothing to help her current quandary much, either. About all she knew for certain was that there was definitely some mystic force at work regarding her attraction to Cale which defied reason or common sense.

Since she'd first laid eyes on the man, she'd been experiencing a serious case of lust. A crook she might be, but she didn't believe for a second she had the capacity to lie to herself. Which left her with one more problem on her growing list, what did she do now?

By the time they'd reached the ugly turquoise staircase, she hadn't come to any conclusions where Cale was concerned. In fact, she was feeling more than a little irritated with him. She'd been honest with him, told him what could very well be the truth about who she might be, and he had the audacity to behave as if she'd just told him she was the next in line to the throne of England.

"I don't know why you think my being a criminal is so damned funny," she muttered as she waited for him to open the door.

He glanced over his shoulder at her as he reached

for the doorknob. "Because it *is* funny. If you're a criminal, then I'm a Russian spy."

He twisted the knob, but nothing happened. "Did you lock the door?"

"Of course." In her mind, she thought she heard the distinct jingle of keys. Were they hers? She had no idea. "Don't you always lock the door when you leave the house?"

He rattled the doorknob again. "Not when I'm only taking Pearl for a walk, I don't. I'm more worried about losing my keys on the beach than about anyone breaking into this place."

"You must have a spare key hidden somewhere."

He shook his head. "Nope."

Maggie stepped in front of him and held out her good hand. "Give me one of your credit cards."

He frowned, but dug into his hip pocket and retrieved his wallet, slipping a gold card from the holder. "What do you think you're doing?"

"Watch, Agent-Perry-ka-nova, and learn." It took her all of two seconds to trip the lock and hand him back his card. "You were saying?" she added smugly as she opened the door.

Cale followed her, let Pearl off her lead then slipped out of his leather jacket without a word. He stared at Maggie as if seeing her for the first time. She had no idea where or how she'd learned to pick a lock, but in her opinion, it only confirmed her suspicion that she and the justice system operated on opposing sides.

Eventually, Cale shook his head. "No," he said. "You could've learned that anywhere."

"Maybe," she admitted with a shrug. "But I don't think so."

"If you were a crook, would you really be so willing to contact the authorities?"

She thought about that for a second while she removed the jacket Cale had lent her. Would she?

There were no easy answers, and the ones she continued to come up with weren't exactly what she wanted to hear, either.

She dropped down on the sofa and toed off her sneakers. "Maybe because that bump on the head put me in my right mind."

Cale chuckled again. "I think you've been watching too much daytime television."

She tucked her feet beneath her and reached for the closest throw pillow to hug to her chest. "Why is it so hard to believe?" she asked him again. "You just saw for yourself what happened on the beach. And, why would I be having these dreams if there wasn't some truth to them? Nothing else makes any sense."

He walked to the sofa and sat beside her. She wished he'd sit elsewhere. When he was so close, she had a hard time keeping her thoughts in order.

"You mean you've had more than just one?"

She nodded. "In the hospital. All I can remember are bits and pieces, but there is a connection."

She explained the images she recalled from the dreams, reluctantly admitting to him about the safe and her knowledge of high-tech security systems, as well as the strange red-silk hankie business. However, nothing explained her reaction to the backfiring car.

She looked over at Cale. "I can still hear it. That sound, like a loud crack or maybe a gunshot. It's constant, almost timed." This time, though, she knew it was only in her mind, teasing her memory. Except now the sound was more rhythmic, familiar and nowhere near as threatening.

Cale moved closer to her side.

"There's a rhythm." She tried to grasp the visions teasing her subconscious, but they remained hidden in souplike fog. "A beat. No. Wait. It's more like a constant clicking."

His hand slid down her arm, stopping at the ridge of her cast. "Do you know where you are? If you close your eyes, can you recognize your surroundings?"

The minute she lowered her lids, the crackling noise stilled and slipped back into the shadows of her mind, into that place the doctors assured her would reopen in time.

She tossed the pillow aside then pulled her knees up to her chest, wrapping her arms around her calves. Resting her chin on her upraised knees, she looked back at Cale. A frown sharpened the lines of his handsome face, a look more angular and rough than she'd seen.

"It's gone," she told him, fighting back an unexpected wave of self-pity and irritation. Dammit, why couldn't she remember anything? "Whatever it is, it's gone now."

"We're pushing too hard," he said gently. "It'll come to you when the time is right."

Irritation nipped at her. Hard. She pulled away from him and stood, circling the coffee table before coming to a stop. "How much time, Cale? A week? A month? How about a year, or maybe two or three?" She struggled to hold on to a temper she hadn't even realized existed. What she really wanted to do was rail in frustration.

Compassion lined his gaze. "You don't know that." The reasonableness of his tone set her teeth on edge.

She pulled in a deep breath in an effort to calm herself. "If I can't rediscover my life, I'm going to have to create a new one. I'm going to need a *legitimate* job, a place to live, although that's a little hard when I don't even know my last name. I haven't a clue if I'm educated or if I wasn't any more ambitious than the fry girl at a fast-food chain. And who exactly do you think is going to hire me? Even burger joints would be a little suspicious of an applicant over the age of sixteen without an employment history."

"You're not going to remember this way," he argued, not the least put out by her sarcastic rant. "You can't keep beating yourself up every time a memory, if that's what they really are, slips away from you." The man even had the gall to grant her another one of his sexy little smiles, which only served to start her pulse revving again.

"It's getting late," he added. "Why don't we get you settled for the night and we can worry about the missing pieces later, okay?"

More irritating than his logical tone was the way he continued to humor her. Okay, so maybe he was right, and she wasn't going to recover her memory by standing in the middle of his living room having herself a well-deserved snit. That didn't mean she had to like it.

"Missing pieces," she muttered and shook her head. "How about a missing life?"

"You can't force something that isn't there, Maggie. And worrying about it won't bring it back any sooner, especially when it only upsets you. Speaking as a medical professional—"

"It's more than just pieces," she interrupted. "My *life*, my entire *history* is gone."

He let out a long breath. "You have to give it time." His voice was the epitome of calm. She vaguely recalled the moments after the explosion. Cale's soothing voice reassuring her she'd be fine, that he'd take care of her. Well, she was tired of calm. She was tired of reassurances. Dammit, she wanted answers that made sense.

She attempted to cross her arms, but the cumbersome cast made it too uncomfortable, so she gave him a steely look instead. "You have family, right?" she asked, indicating the half dozen or so framed photographs artfully arranged on the wall above a beautifully crafted rolltop desk.

"Yeah, so?"

"So? Who are they? What are their names?"

He gave her a questioning look before he stood and crossed the room. "This is Drew. He's my younger brother," he said, pointing to a photograph of himself with two other men sharing a strong family resemblance. All three of them were in uniform, standing in front of a bright red fire truck. "And Ben, he's the oldest."

He pointed to another photograph depicting a middle-aged woman, handsomely dressed with gently graying hair and soft blue eyes filled with laughter. She stood proudly beneath a Grand Opening sign in front of a bookstore. "That's my aunt who raised us after my folks died."

He pulled down a photograph and handed it to her. It was a black-and-white wedding photo Maggie gauged to be close to forty years old by the way the bride and groom were dressed. They stood on the beach, barefoot, with their backs to the ocean. Cale's mother wore a white, gauzy gown and a floral wreath in her long, dark hair, and his dad was dressed casually in jeans and a tie-dyed T-shirt, a couple of strings of love beads around his neck. But what struck Maggie hardest was the sheer happiness on the couple's faces. Something nudged her mind, but the harder she attempted to grasp the memory, the farther it slipped away from her.

"There are a couple of uncles I haven't seen in years," he said, returning the photograph to its place on the wall. "You want to tell me what your point is?"

"Humor me a minute," she said. "What about grandparents? Did you know your grandparents?"

A deep frown furrowed his forehead. "Only a grandmother on my mom's side that we used to visit about once a year when we were kids. My dad's folks passed away before I was born. I don't understand what you're looking for."

She ceased her rapid-fire interrogation and hoped she could make him understand how alone she truly was in the world until her memory came back to her. "You know all those people in these pictures," she said with a sweep of her hand. "Can you try for just one minute to imagine what it would be like to know nothing about your family, not even to know if you have a family? How do you think you'd feel if you knew absolutely nothing about yourself or where you came from?"

He stared at her for the space of a few heartbeats, then slowly closed the distance separating them. Gently, he lifted his hand to slip a lock of hair behind her ear. "I think I understand what you're trying to tell me."

The care in his touch stirred something deep inside her, stroked that place where she knew her attraction to Cale was a good thing, no matter what condition her life might be in at the moment.

His palm cupped her cheek, warm, comforting. And distracting as hell.

"When you keep trying to force yourself to remember," he said, "and then you aren't able to, you're not helping yourself. I know I pushed you earlier, and I shouldn't have. I should know better, and I'm sorry."

The urge to turn into the warmth of his hand was strong. Right or wrong, no matter how much she yearned for the comfort, she restrained herself. Allowing herself to become dependent on Cale was nothing short of emotional suicide, and she'd already pushed the boundaries of what remained of her emotional well-being with that kiss.

With more reluctance than she thought possible, she pulled away from him. Her world had been turned upside down enough for one night. With her life already being such a puzzle, and with a whole host of missing pieces yet to be found, she refused to compound her problems by relying on anyone other than herself. At least emotionally. For the time being, she did physically need his help, and while that made it hard to be independent, she had little choice in the matter.

For now.

With luck, she'd find the remaining pieces of her life on her own, and she deeply suspected those odd dreams were the key to only one small segment of her former reality. If she failed to find the pieces, she'd simply have to create new ones.

Again. Part of her knew she'd had to do it before.

She attempted to push that last disturbing thought aside for the moment. "Then please, stop telling me to relax and not worry. I am worried. I have two choices right now. I can either attempt to reconstruct my previous life, or I'll have to make up a new one. I don't even know where the closest cemetery is to go traipsing among the headstones looking for..."

*Oh, my God.* Looking for what? A name? An identity she could...*steal?*

Cale stared at her, disbelief etched all over his handsome face. He blew out a long breath, then shoved his hand through his black hair. "What are you talking about?"

The caution in his voice didn't surprise her in the least, but she was too stunned by her own revelation to give much thought to his reaction.

She took several steps backward until her fanny

brushed against the front door. Breathing suddenly took eons of effort, becoming more and more difficult with every breath she attempted to drag into her lungs. Her legs went weak and nearly gave out on her. Using the flat of her palm of her good hand, she braced it against the smooth wooden door for support.

She shook her head. "No. I don't think I want to know any more about Maggie," she murmured. "I don't like what I'm learning."

If the glimpse she'd just caught was any indication of her true identity, maybe losing her memory was the best thing that had ever happened to her. The more she discovered, the less she liked herself. First she was a thief of some sort, and now she might have a false identity? How on earth was she supposed to find herself if all she had to follow was a list of aliases?

She wrapped her arms around her middle and leaned forward, the cast on her arm pressing painfully into her stomach. Jeez Louise, she was confused. Was any of it real? It had to be, the memories were simply too clear to be anything else.

She glanced at Cale. He hadn't moved, just stood there in the middle of the living room, staring at her as if seeing her for the first time. Not that she blamed him. She could hardly believe what she'd just learned herself.

"Back up a minute," he said, his voice filled with caution. "Are you implying you know how to create a false identity?"

The hairs on the back of her neck stood at attention. Dread filled her body as she slowly nodded.

"LaRue," she whispered.

"What?"

She cleared her suddenly clogged throat. "LaRue," she repeated with more force. "My name is Maggie LaRue."

"How do you know?"

She straightened and gave him a level stare. "Because I got it off a headstone."

# 7

AFTER SPENDING a restless night haunted by his own bizarre dreams, Cale slowly stepped into his jeans then pulled a T-shirt from the basket of unfolded laundry. He still hadn't come to terms with Maggie's strange revelation. In fact, he couldn't even say that he believed her. Truth, as the saying went, may indeed be stranger than fiction, but Maggie was no crook, no matter what strange and unusual scenarios popped into her head. That she'd been appalled by the revelations spoke volumes about her sense of morality and character.

As he left his bedroom and headed into the kitchen in search of much-needed caffeine, the soft, gentle sound of feminine laughter caught him off guard. Finding her in a light and happy mood was nowhere near what he expected after last night's discussion about her creating a false identity or two in the past. He'd figured she might be feeling more than a little morose this morning. Contemplative and worried, definitely. But cheery? Not in a million.

The enticing aromas of frying bacon and blessed coffee met him as he crossed the living room in his bare feet. He couldn't help the smile that tugged his lips. Apparently Maggie possessed other talents, as well. Thank heaven for both of them, cooking had made the list.

He slipped into the kitchen and stopped when he spotted Drew in front of the stove shuffling a fry pan filled with potatoes, onions and bell peppers. Maggie leaned against the counter, smiling at Drew with a definite sparkle in her eyes.

The sharp twist in Cale's gut was not jealousy, he told himself. So what if his brother was smiling like a fool at his...at Maggie?

He shoved his hand through his hair. "What are you doing here?" he groused at his brother.

Drew glanced over his shoulder at him and his smile deepened. "Fixing breakfast. What does it look like?"

It looked as if he was flirting with Maggie.

Cale glanced at the clock above the sink. Seven-thirty? In the morning? On a Saturday? "I meant what are you doing here so early?"

Drew set the pan back on the stove, covered it with a lid, then lowered the flame. "I brought groceries." He produced a carton of eggs from the refrigerator as proof. "You don't want your houseguest starving to death, do you?"

And here Cale had thought Ben was the only brother to constantly stick his nose where it wasn't wanted. "I planned on going to the store before my shift tonight."

Drew shrugged. "You still need to," he said, returning his attention to the frying bacon. "I only picked up enough to make breakfast."

Cale looked around the clutter in his small kitchen.

More like enough to make breakfast for a small army. Which could only mean Ben would be arriving shortly.

Maggie turned and reached into the cabinet for another mug. His gaze zeroed in on the curve of her backside and the way the charcoal-gray top he'd picked up for her crept up, exposing smooth, creamy flesh above the waistband of her jeans. "You didn't tell me your brother was a minor gourmet." She filled the mug with coffee and handed it to Cale.

He grunted in response. Drew did enjoy cooking, especially for beautiful women. He always figured it was his brother's idea of foreplay.

With that thought blossoming like ragweed in his mind, Cale shifted his gaze from Maggie to Drew and back again until it finally dawned on him that Maggie had dressed herself. How was that possible? Yesterday she'd been near tears because she hadn't been able to manage on her own. Now she wasn't just dressed, but damned chipper besides? He was *not* jealous. Even if Cale was powerless to prevent the nagging suspicion that perhaps his overly chivalrous brother had arrived early enough to help her into her clothes, he was not falling victim to something as petty as jealousy.

His gut twisted again, making a liar out of him. Dammit.

"Any problems this morning?" he asked Maggie, throwing in a determined sweep of his gaze down her alluring body for good measure.

Her eyes widened in surprise, then narrowed slightly. The gold rim surrounding her irises came to life, adding just the right amount of spark to set his pulse into overdrive.

"Nothing that a little ingenuity didn't solve." Her sharp tone let him know loud and clear she'd picked up on his meaning, and that she didn't appreciate the Neanderthal routine.

Was it his fault he was feeling a little... Okay so he was jealous. There. He admitted it. Shoot him. Not that he had any right to those feelings, but after the way Maggie had kissed him, he couldn't stop himself. Apparently, his body had staked a claim, even if his mind had yet to fully slip around the idea.

He ignored Drew's questioning look as he took his coffee and strode into the breakfast area to see to Gilda before he made an even bigger fool of himself. Maggie's life was in enough turmoil without him complicating matters. Besides, once her memory returned, she'd be gone. History. Adios, baby. Yup, Maggie LaRue would be just one more in a relatively moderate line of women he'd stepped forward to assist in one way or another. Nothing more. Nothing less.

Now *that* he needed to remember, not the way her body had arched against his, or the way her lips had parted, welcoming him inside. While he was at it, he'd better forget about the feel of her satiny-smooth skin beneath his hands, too.

Maybe, if he tried hard enough, and was damned lucky, he just might pull it off.

*Yeah? And who do you think you're kidding, pal?*

He slipped the cover from Gilda's cage and tucked it on the shelf beneath. The big bird ruffled her bright-colored feathers and squawked, followed by the sound of a rich purr that would've made Mae West proud. "Hello, lover."

Although still a bit too crude for polite company, at least the old gal was getting better at realizing her own gender. Half the time she greeted him like a drunken sailor requesting a sexual favor.

"Good morning, Gilda. Sleep well?"

Gilda squawked in response, then bobbed up and down, anxious for her favorite morning treat of fresh grapes. Since he hadn't been to the store in nearly a week, dry fruit-flavored cereal rings would have to placate her for the time being. If they didn't, then Lord only knew what vile words she'd spout to voice her displeasure.

He took care cleaning Gilda's cage, wandering back and forth between the kitchen and the morning room. With each trip, his awareness of Maggie heightened. The way her eyes met and held his. The slight blush that stained her cheeks when he caught her staring at him when she thought he wasn't paying attention. The sweet sound of her voice as she carried on a conversation about books with Drew. The soft, alluring scent of her.

He refilled Gilda's bowl with her daily feed, dropped a few bits of cereal in a second bowl, then carried them back for Gilda's inspection. The parrot showed her appreciation by hanging off the side of her cage and belting out a couple of bars of "Peggy Sue."

Something about Maggie had changed since last night, he realized as he snapped Gilda's bowls back into their holders. An air of self-assurance that had been hiding beneath the surface all along, perhaps? He'd already determined the woman possessed an independent streak a mile wide. Nor did she bully easily, as evidenced by the way she'd held her own against those two detectives who had questioned her. But why all of a sudden, he wondered? What had changed in the last nine hours or so?

The exact answer evaded him as he returned to the kitchen to retrieve from the pantry the bottled water he kept on hand for Gilda.

"Oh, my God!" Maggie exclaimed suddenly. "I remember reading that book."

Cale straightened. "What book?" The sheer delight on her face made him smile.

Drew slung the dishtowel he'd been using as a pot holder over his shoulder, then poured himself another cup of coffee. *"Fahrenheit 451."*

Cale vaguely recalled the story. "Something about burning books?"

Maggie's grin widened. "Sort of," she said, her excitement palpable. "It's more about censorship and the deterioration of a society obsessed with visual medium."

"What else have you read?" He kept his tone casual, hoping to not appear as if her answers held any more value than a discussion of reading tastes.

A slight frown marred her forehead for the space of two heartbeats. "William Faulkner." Her smile slowly returned. "His Snopes trilogy and *As I Lay Dying.* George Orwell. *1984. Animal Farm.* I can't believe

I remember this," she said, her voice filling with laughter.

Drew cast a quick glance in Cale's direction, then walked back to the stove to remove the bacon from the pan. "Doesn't sound like reading for pleasure to me."

Cale set the water container on the counter, then crossed his arms over his chest. "That's because your idea of literary fiction comes in a plain brown wrapper."

No one could ever accuse Drew of being dense. Despite his nonchalance, he obviously understood the importance of the small snippet of information for Maggie and strove to keep the conversation flowing in case another revelation surfaced.

She pushed away from the counter and shook her head. "It wasn't for pleasure," she said, her tone turning cautious. Her eyes took on the same faraway look she'd had when she'd announced she'd gotten her name from a headstone.

She tilted her head slightly to the side. "It was for a paper that I wrote comparing *As I Lay Dying* to Chaucer's *Canterbury Tales*. I focused on the pilgrimage theme in both books."

Drew shot Cale a knowing look. "That doesn't sound like any high-school paper I ever wrote."

Her lips thinned into a grim line as she reached deep inside her cloudy mind for the memory. "That's because I wrote it in college." She focused her attention on Cale. "Do you know what this means?"

"That you went to college." Nothing like stating the obvious.

Her nod was as cautious as her tone, as if she didn't quite trust the memory. "Do you realize what my chances are of finding out where?"

Zip to none, he thought, understanding her reluctance to celebrate this latest discovery. Contacting the thousands of colleges and universities across the nation would be a task nothing short of daunting, not to mention the possibility that Maggie LaRue might not even exist, except as a figment of her faulty imagination.

"About as likely as finding a woman in Southern California that Drew hasn't dated," he said, hoping to lighten her mood again.

The doorbell rang, signaling Ben's arrival. Drew tossed the dishtowel at Cale good-naturedly. "You're a real comedian," he said, then went to open the door.

Maggie rewarded Cale's attempt at levity with the barest hint of a smile as she digested the new minute detail of her past. While a welcome change from all those hints of a nefarious lifestyle, the fact remained that this single piece of the larger puzzle provided little help in determining her identity.

"Breakfast is nearly ready," she said, unwilling to face yet another postmortem. "I'll set the table."

She opened the cabinet where she'd spied the plates when she'd been searching for coffee mugs earlier and lifted up on her toes to reach the shelf. A large, warm hand settled on her hip. She didn't need to look to know that Cale had moved in behind her. The stuttering of her pulse gave off more than enough warning of his nearness.

"Let me." The low husky rumble of his voice near

her ear stirred her senses. Not that they'd been all that dormant since he'd strolled into the kitchen wearing a pair of faded jeans and a lazy bedroom smile.

She was, after all, a red-blooded woman. What was she supposed to do if her hormones whipped into a frenzy whenever she dared to look at the way the snug denim clung to his lean hips and strong thighs? The heather-gray-and-navy-baseball-style T-shirt outlining his powerful chest and wide shoulders hardly helped matters, either. Just the idea of taming her more base instincts was downright laughable.

If she didn't divert her eyes from the way the muscles in his forearms corded as he lifted the heavy stoneware plates from the shelf, the odds of her actually having to wipe drool from her chin doubled by the second.

"Thank you." Despite being surrounded by all that distracting maleness, her vocal chords were at least operational. "I can take it from here."

Using her cast for additional support, she scooped up the plates and scooted into the sunny breakfast nook. She refused to think of her abrupt retreat as anything but self-preservation of what little common sense she had left. Unfortunately, where Cale was concerned, hers had apparently gone AWOL.

She didn't have time to bemoan that little fact of life. Cale's oldest brother had arrived, Drew proclaimed breakfast ready and Gilda had decided now was as good a time as any to serenade them with snippets of Elvis and Buddy.

She enjoyed the delicious breakfast and listened as Cale and his brothers gently teased one another and talked about people and places that held no meaning for her. As she bit into her second flaky, buttery croissant, a quiet sense of longing slipped over her. The feeling no doubt stemmed from the carefree camaraderie Cale shared with his siblings, however, she hadn't expected the familiarity of the emotion. It was as if she'd experienced the sensation many times over the years.

"So what can you tell me about yourself, Maggie?"

Her hand, holding a knife with a small slab of butter on it, stilled in mid-air. Ben's abrupt question not only took her by complete surprise, but she detected thinly veiled suspicion, as well. Hadn't Cale told his oldest brother about her lack of memory?

The smile she attempted felt more like a grimace of pain. "Seems that's the question of the hour."

Ben nodded slowly, then lifted the porcelain mug of coffee to his lips. His chilled, icy-blue eyes never left her face.

Cale let out a rough sigh and pushed his plate away. "Real subtle, Ben."

"Don't take it personally, Maggie," Drew told her. "Ben is under the misguided belief that everyone else's business is his."

"It's a curse," Cale added, and shot a dark, warning look at his older brother.

Rather than comment, Drew downed the juice in his glass.

Ben's expression softened only slightly. "I apologize, Maggie. I didn't mean—"

"Look, it's okay." She meant it, too, knowing she'd consider herself lucky if someone in her life cared about her the way Ben obviously did his brothers. "What do you want to know?"

He pushed aside his own empty plate and leaned forward, bracing his arms on the table. "Anything that might help us determine your identity."

She laid her knife on the edge of her plate along with the uneaten croissant. "Well—"

"She doesn't remember much of anything," Cale interrupted. "So don't go upsetting her by reminding her of that fact."

Drew used his fork to toy with the remnants of the hash browns on his plate. "He's got a point, Ben."

She appreciated Cale, and even Drew, coming to her defense, but dammit, she was really getting a little tired of being treated like a delicate china doll that would shatter if anyone spoke a harsh word to her. Worse, she realized with sudden clarity, since she'd awoken in the hospital, she'd done her part by letting herself play the role of victim.

Well, no more. Whether she'd ever make a full recovery remained as much a mystery as her past, but that most certainly did not render her incapable of facing her future. The time had come for Maggie LaRue to stand up and take charge.

So she couldn't remember anything significant about her life. She wouldn't allow her situation to provide her with a license to depend on anyone but herself. And she could start by defending herself in the face of Ben's understated cross-examination.

She pulled in a deep breath and gave Ben a level stare. "My name is Maggie LaRue, but I doubt it's really mine." The careless shrug was just an act, but it worked for her. "I believe I may have taken the name off a headstone."

Drew coughed, nearly choking on his last slice of bacon.

"Maggie, don't—"

She lifted her hand to stop Cale before he said anything further. With determined bravado, she settled back against the tropical-print cushion, crossed her legs and addressed Ben. "As of this morning I'm pretty sure I went to college."

Ben shrugged. "Which means you're probably a little overqualified for a career in ditch-digging."

Her courage slipped a notch when she felt a flash of irritation, demanding attention. Whether it stemmed from Ben's tone or her own growing frustration over her lack of solid answers, she didn't much care.

"I have a feeling that William Faulkner is one of my favorite authors, and that I prefer books to movies or television, but I do have an appreciation for anything by Ibsen or Tennessee Williams. I also believe I have firsthand knowledge of firearms and security systems."

Cale cleared his throat, either distressed by her behavior, or concerned over his brother's stoic reaction to her last bombshell. "Maggie, don't do this."

Foolish or not, she ignored his warning. "I also know what I don't like."

Her gaze connected with Cale's, allowing him to gauge her mood. At least the man had the good sense to remain silent.

"I don't like being told what to do," she said, giving each brother a pointed stare. "While I do appreciate the concern, I most certainly do not welcome being coddled. And I especially don't like not knowing who I really am or where the..." She pulled in a deep breath, then let it out slowly in an effort to cool her rising temper. "Or where it is I come from," she finished in a gentler tone.

She shifted her gaze back to Cale's older brother. "That's it," she told him. "That's all I know. I'm open to suggestions, but you should know that it's a pretty good bet I don't appreciate people meddling in my life, either."

Ben's icy gaze filled with something she suspected just might be grudging respect. A small grin tipped the corner of his mouth, confirming her suspicions. "Such as it is," he said, after a moment.

She let out the breath she'd been holding and returned his smile with a brief one of her own. "Yes. Such as it is."

Something passed between Cale and his younger brother, a look that spoke a silent language she understood nothing about. "You forgot something," Cale told her.

Drew attempted unsuccessfully to smother a laugh. "Boy, I'll say."

"And?" she prompted when the brothers exchanged yet another conspiratorial look.

"Temper," Cale said, a teasing expression entering his heavenly blue eyes.

"Should've known," Drew added with a shake of his head.

Ben chuckled. "It's the hair," he said, then actually winked at her.

Cale snapped his fingers. "A dead giveaway. How did I miss that?"

Relieved that the tension had finally passed, Maggie rolled her eyes, then stood and started collecting the dishes. Chairs scraped against the tile floor as the Perry men rose from the table. Drew and Ben made a hasty escape on the ruse of examining the latest renovation on the house, leaving her and Cale alone to clean up the mess.

"Like rats deserting a sinking ship," Cale called after his brothers.

"I should probably apologize," she said, gathering the silverware. "I didn't mean to lose it like that."

Cale circled the table and took the silverware from her, depositing it inside an empty glass. The gentleness of his touch as he settled his big hands on her shoulders and turned her to face him, warmed her from the inside out. The man was simply too dangerous. Not only to her senses, but to her newly discovered—or resurrected—determination to depend on no one but herself.

One of those seductive little half smiles tipped the corner of his mouth, weakening her resolve. "I wouldn't worry too much about it." His hands slowly inched toward her neck. "If Ben and Drew were in your shoes, I'd bet their ability to hold back their frustration would be nonexistent."

From the way the tips of her breasts were tingling in response to the seductive brush of Cale's thumbs against her throat, her frustration had stretched to astronomical proportions, the kind that would take a cold shower to ebb.

The base of his thumb pressed against her rapidly beating pulse, revealing to him just how much he physically affected her. His eyes darkened, desire simmering in the depths, intoxicating her.

"Besides," he murmured, his voice smooth and more enticing than a hot fudge sundae. "We've already determined you couldn't possibly help yourself."

"I couldn't?"

His hand slid into her hair, lifting the heavy weight from the back of her neck. "No," he said. "Not with you being a redhead and all."

With every single ounce of willpower she possessed, she stepped back, hoping to break the sensual spell Cale so effortlessly wove around her. Her hands trembled as she lifted the stack of plates from the table, the rattle sounding louder than an explosion of dynamite.

Cale's all too knowing chuckle instantly brought out the wickedness in her. Yes, he affected her. His touch, his voice, the way his eyes went from sky blue to navy when he looked at her in that certain way. All of it, all of him, left her body humming with awareness and a deep, aching need. Didn't he deserve to experience a small taste of the same blissful torture himself?

She shoved the plates toward him, giving him no choice but to take them from her or let them crash to the floor. She spun on her heel and headed toward the kitchen, stopping when she reached the arch separating the two rooms. With a deliberate shake of her hair, she looked over her shoulder and gave him what she hoped was a smoldering look filled with sin.

"Cale?" she called quietly to him, with just enough of a husky undertone to make him wary.

Her ploy worked.

Apprehension and wonderment crossed his handsome face. "Yeah?" The sound was definitely strained.

Enjoying the game, she deliberately moistened her bottom lip with her tongue. "That's only the case if I'm a true redhead."

Ceramic clattered and rattled as Cale struggled to keep the plates from slipping out of his hands as her meaning penetrated. He clutched the dishes to his chest, then swore when the remnants of their breakfast smeared over his shirt.

"You cheat, sweetheart." A definite warning filled with sensual intent lined his tone and ignited her imagination.

She laughed, knowing without a doubt she was playing with fire, but the slow burn of desire in the pit of her tummy was too intoxicating for her to walk away now.

"You sure you want to play this game?"

The wicked grin on his face should have scared her off, but instead of hightailing it to safety, she deliberately crossed the kitchen toward him. "When I play," she told him, "I play to win."

His laughter warmed her as he set the dishes on the counter. He turned and slowly peeled the filthy T-shirt over his head, revealing, inch by delicious inch, his well-tanned, muscular torso.

She itched to smooth her hands over the texture of his skin, to press her lips to that glorious wall of flesh. As she wrestled with the wisdom of her actions, he tossed the shirt aside and reached for her. With his hands locked firmly on the swell of her hips, he backed her up against the refrigerator and pressed his body into hers.

"So do I," he whispered, his breath hot against her ear. "And I won't lose."

The snappy comeback hovering on her lips vanished the second his tongue traced the outline of her ear, and she trembled. "Who's cheating now?" she managed, her voice a strained whisper. "Ooh, I can't think when you do that."

"I don't want you to think, Maggie. I want you to feel."

His mouth caught hers, stealing her breath and sending her hormones into a messy tangle. This was no soft brush of the lips, but a kiss totally consuming and filled with enough heat to melt her on the spot.

His hands left her hips, wandering up her sides where his thumbs settled below her breasts. Her nipples beaded, anticipating his touch. The ache between her legs increased, so she pressed her thighs together to quiet the slow, steady throb. Her tongue mated with his and she gave in to the desire to explore the landscape of his body with her good hand.

A whole lot sooner than she was ready for, he ended the kiss. He rested his forehead against hers, his uneven breaths teasing her tingling lips.

What on earth was she thinking? Cale Perry was

definitely too hot for her to handle. But no way was she about to let on how much he'd just rattled her.

Needing distance, she eased away from him. "Are you any good at crossword puzzles?" she asked him, determined to end this encounter in her favor. No matter how much of a hero complex he might suffer from, or how chivalrous his nature, she didn't doubt for a second that she would easily find her heart charred beyond recognition if she wasn't careful.

With his hands braced against the fridge as if he needed the support, he looked over his shoulder. "Why?" he asked with a hefty dose of caution.

She summoned up a saucy smile in hopes of convincing him of a confidence she was nowhere near feeling. "What's a three-letter word that starts with *W* for aroused?"

He hesitated a moment, then shook his head.

Deliberately, she slowly moistened her lips. *"Wet."* She gave him a last sassy wink and walked away, the echo from his groan of pure agony doing wonders for her ego.

# 8

CALE TWISTED the cold tap to full blast. The icy spray had zero effect on his current state of arousal. Even the scandalous images Maggie's provocative parting shot evoked in his mind refused to stand down in the face of a freezing shower.

He'd cleaned up the kitchen, alone, in ten minutes, then beelined it to the shower in hopes of quelling the erotic thoughts, and his body's rock-hard reaction.

No such luck.

The memory of the sexy glint in Maggie's eyes stubbornly refused banishment from his mind. The seductive tone of her voice as she'd uttered that one fantasy-inducing word still rang in his ears. Not even the reminder that he and Maggie weren't alone had the power to bring his testosterone down to a manageable level.

*Face it, pal, you're screwed.*

He muttered a curse, along with a reluctant agreement, then dipped his head beneath the shower nozzle. There were days when he really hated the direct honesty of his conscience. Today was no exception.

His body ached for her, and no amount of cold water could dispel that fact. He'd kissed her, tasted those honey-sweet lips, had felt her tongue tangle with his and he wanted more. She had him so twisted in knots with wanting her, he was close to ignoring the reasons why he should keep his hands to himself.

He wanted her in his bed. Just the thought of the soft, sultry moans she'd make when he pleasured her had him cranking the cold water tap to high. The heavy blast failed to cool the need burning in his gut or quell the desire to feel her body beneath his.

He was a powder keg of need, he thought as he shut off the water and stepped from the shower. Ready to explode. Maggie not only held the match, the woman was setting off dangerous sparks.

He dried off and dressed quickly, then headed downstairs to join Maggie and his brothers in the room that would become his den if he ever got around to finishing it. As the largest room in the house, it had required the most work. He'd gutted it, hauling away old plaster, replaced the aging studs with new lumber and updated the area with drywall and a coffered ceiling. Over the last two years, room by room, he'd slowly been turning his investment into an attractive piece of beach property. He figured after another couple of years, he'd be ready to put the house on the market, make a decent profit, he hoped, then start the process all over again with another fixer-upper he could purchase for a song.

The room was empty, but the sliding glass doors leading into the backyard stood open. He followed the sound of voices and stepped through the doors onto the patio slab he'd replaced shortly after the spring rains.

Like a magnet, he was instantly drawn to Maggie.

She sat on the bench at the redwood picnic table near the edge of the covered patio, her injured arm resting on the top. The rich cinnamon of her hair gleamed in the morning sunshine. His fingers itched to lift the reddish strands and let them sift through his fingers.

Her provocative taunt slammed into him. If only they were alone.

Drew and Ben had commandeered the white plastic patio chairs, neither of them in any apparent hurry to leave. Which was probably for the best, Cale thought as he crossed the patio to the picnic table. His ability to maintain a respectable distance from Maggie hovered in the dangerously low to nonexistent category.

Cale thumbed his nose at his rapidly dwindling self-control and sat down on the bench beside Maggie. Pearl trotted over and dropped her big black head on his knee in a bid for attention. He absently petted the dog's neck.

"Weren't you scheduled to work today?" he asked Ben, not that he was trying to get his brothers to leave or anything.

"I go on at midnight," Ben answered with a brief shake of his head. "Trinity's shorthanded this weekend, so I'm pulling a thirty-six-hour shift."

Drew cast a knowing look in Cale's direction. "I think he's trying to get rid of us."

Was he really that transparent? Apparently so, if the smirk on Drew's face was any indication.

Out of the corner of his eye, Cale caught sight of the slight blush coloring Maggie's cheeks. Damn, but she was cute. And one hell of a contradiction that had nothing whatsoever to do with her peculiar past. The mysteries he wanted, no, *needed* to solve stemmed from discovering which woman was the heart of the real Maggie LaRue: the woman who blushed prettily at a relatively innocent innuendo, or the captivating siren who'd nearly sent him to his knees ready to beg for the privilege of uncovering all of her sensual secrets.

She adjusted the position of her arm on the table. He didn't miss the slight wince that briefly tugged her eyebrows into a frown. "Trinity?" she asked Ben. "I thought you guys worked for the Los Angeles County Fire Department."

"Trinity Station," Drew said. "It's a nickname."

Ben leaned back in the chair and laced his fingers over his stomach. Nope. His brothers were definitely not going anywhere anytime soon.

"The intersection where the firehouse is located is surrounded by three churches," Ben explained. "Station 43 is on one corner. St. Jude's Catholic Church and their private school on another, with Santa Monica Methodist and Community Baptist taking the other two."

"The patron saint of lost causes," she murmured. "I think I've been praying to the wrong deity."

"Either you studied theology or you're Catholic," Drew said.

Maggie frowned, then shrugged. "Maybe," she said thoughtfully. "Tell me about Trinity."

Drew picked up the large red rubber doggy toy lying on the white plastic table between the two chairs. He tossed it up and down, instantly drawing Pearl's attention. "The house has been called Trinity Station for as long as I can remember."

No longer interested in love and affection when there was a warm body around willing to toss her favorite toy, Pearl deserted Cale.

"How is it all three of you work at the same station together?" Maggie asked.

Drew chucked the toy across the yard. "Dumb luck," he said, but there was a hint of pride evident in his voice. "We don't always work the same shifts though. And I don't have the squirrelly hours these guys have to put up with half the time. Except for the occasional call when I'm off duty, I'm pretty much a part of the nine-to-five crowd."

Cale understood Drew's reasons for going into arson investigation. He'd been one hell of a firefighter, but after the death of one of their own during a three-alarm blaze a few years ago, Drew quickly put in for a transfer to the arson unit. The truth of the matter was, Drew absolutely detested hospitals, emergency rooms in particular. While an actual firefighter's trips to emergency rooms were minimal compared to that of a paramedic, working with the arson unit generally kept Drew out of the antiseptic halls. The few occasions when he was required to pay a visit to a hospitalized witness, or worse, the morgue, were more than enough for the youngest Perry brother.

Cale leaned back and braced his elbows on the table behind him. "That reminds me," he said, stretching his legs out in front of him. "Were you able to find out anything about the warehouse fire?"

Drew picked up the toy Pearl dropped at his feet

and threw it across the yard again for her. She took off like shot, stirring up dust, grass and leaves as she raced around the avocado tree. The debris fluttered down on Frankie and Johnny who had been napping peacefully beneath the shade of the big tree. Frankie, the more temperamental of the two felines, hissed her displeasure at the disturbance of one of her treasured snoozing sessions.

"No suspicious circumstances, if that's what you mean," Drew said.

Effectively scolded by her feline roommates, Pearl carefully retrieved her toy and walked away from the cats. She flopped down near Ben's chair with a loud sigh that sounded more like a disgusted groan now that she'd been chastised. She rested her big square muzzle protectively over her toy.

"That doesn't make much sense," Maggie said to Drew. "If what you're saying is true, then why was I being grilled by a couple of very unfriendly detectives a few days ago?"

Drew shrugged. "Probably because you were in a place that wasn't only closed to the public, but you were there after hours and there was no sign of forced entry. For the company to collect on the insurance, they need to have a full investigation."

"What was the cause of the fire?" Ben asked.

A loud squawk drifted down from the open window in the morning room. "Pucker up, doll." Gilda squawked again. She let out a very impressive wolf whistle, then belted out a string of curses that had Cale considering going upstairs to close the windows before the neighbors started complaining.

Maggie giggled and shook her head in dismay. "You really need to do something about her vocabulary," she whispered to Cale. "It's embarrassing."

No kidding. "She's a work in progress." Excruciatingly slow progress, at that.

"The cause?" Ben prompted Drew once Gilda had settled down to a bits-and-pieces version of a Sinatra medley.

Drew leaned forward and braced his elbows on his knees. "An electrical short in the air-conditioning system. The place was full of accelerants, considering the product it warehoused."

Ben shifted his gaze in Maggie's direction. "You have no idea why you were there?"

Maggie let out a sigh before she answered. "No," she told them. "None whatsoever. I can't even imagine why I would be in a place like that. Detective Villanueva wasn't too impressed with my answers, either."

"I wouldn't worry too much about the cops," Drew said, in an attempt to reassure her. "They're only doing their job."

A shadow passed through Maggie's eyes. "They still made me feel like I was a suspect. Or worse." The fingers peeking out from the cast curled tightly. Her knuckles turned white.

Her distress offered yet another reason Cale had a hard time believing the unusual memories she'd been having. Despite what he'd witnessed of Maggie's behavior, he still held out hope for a logical explanation. Yet, after the incident on the beach followed by her break-and-enter trick with a credit card, even he'd experienced a few misgivings of his own. She'd learned her B-and-E talent somewhere, but he couldn't think of a single college course that taught those skills.

He stood abruptly, eager for a change of subject that would chase away the tension he sensed building inside her again. Her doctor had insisted she rest and try to keep the stress to a minimum. Since he'd brought her home with him from the hospital, they'd both been guilty of ignoring doctor's orders.

"Unless we plan to starve ourselves all week," he said, "maybe we should get the shopping out of the way before I go on duty tonight."

Drew, nowhere near his usual deliberately obtuse self, took the hint and stood. "Good idea. Your cabinets are an embarrassment."

"You working a twenty-four?" Ben asked, following suit.

"No, I've got the six-to-six graveyard tonight with Scorch, then back to days on Monday." He offered his hand to Maggie, but she ignored it and stood on her own. "Do you think you'll be okay by yourself?"

"Of course I will." Her glance was sharp and direct. Those gold rims reappeared in her gaze, letting him know he'd slighted her independence...again. "I'm not a child, Cale."

A detail he was well aware of, in more ways than one. She was a living, breathing, full-grown woman with curves in all the right places. She held the power to turn him inside out with one sassy, sultry look or a husky, feminine laugh. Oh, yeah. She was *all* woman.

"I know that," he said. "It's just...what if you remember something. You probably shouldn't be alone." The last thing he wanted to do was to go into detail in front of his brothers, but he worried she might suffer another recollection of some unpleasant experience trapped in her mind. Was it wrong of him to not want to leave her alone, especially when she might need him?

Drew bent down to pat Pearl's side. "She won't have to be alone tonight."

"I don't need a baby-sitter, either."

"Forget it, Drew," Cale said to his brother. No way was he going to allow his flirtatious little brother to watch over Maggie. "That's like asking a hungry kid to guard the candy store."

"Not me, you idiot," Drew laughed. "Deb and Tilly. Deb made me promise to have you bring Maggie to her place before you go on duty tonight. She called it girls' night. Something about chocolate and old black-and-white movies."

Ben pulled the keys to his pickup from the pocket of his khaki trousers.

"When did you have time to tell Debbie about Maggie?" Cale asked. He'd planned to tell his aunt himself, but wasn't the least bit surprised one of his brothers had beat him to it. A little thing called privacy simply didn't exist in the Perry family.

Drew straightened and retrieved his own set of keys. "Last night. Why?"

"What's this?" Ben teased as they walked toward the side gate. "Friday night and Drew Perry without a date? Or two?"

Drew lightly slugged Ben in the shoulder. "I stopped by before I went out for the night."

"Great," Cale said, relieved Maggie wouldn't be left alone. "Problem solved."

"Excuse me, gentlemen, but there is no problem to be solved." She glared at each of them in turn. "I can take care of myself."

Cale's hand stilled on the gate handle as he exchanged sympathetic glances with his brothers. Great. He'd gone and insulted her again.

"Please thank your aunt for the invitation," she told Drew firmly, "but I'll pass. I wouldn't want to intrude."

Drew slung his arm over Maggie's shoulder. Cale struggled to ignore the sharp twist of his insides at the sight of his brother touching Maggie.

"You might as well agree now, Mags," Drew said with more familiarity than Cale appreciated. "Old Ben here is mild compared to our aunt. Believe me, once she makes up her mind about something, she won't take no for an answer. She has a way of getting people to do what she wants."

Cale nodded quickly in agreement, having been on the receiving end of his aunt's determination on numerous occasions. "If I don't take you over there, Debbie will come here herself and drag you kicking and screaming."

"Not to mention what she'll put Cale through," Ben added with his own conspiratorial nod of agreement.

Maggie squared her shoulders. The defiant lift of her chin made each of them aware she wasn't thrilled with them for ganging up on her.

"Fine. I'll go," she finally relented. She nailed Cale

with her gaze, gold rims and all flaring to life. "And just so you know, I'm agreeing under absolute protest just to save your hide."

His hide, as she put it, wasn't the one in danger. When she looked at him that way, full of fire and sass, her own hide was the one in need of saving. The woman tested the limits of his control. Heaven help them both when the tenuous thread eventually snapped.

AFTER RETURNING from the grocery store with enough food to feed a small army for a month, Cale disappeared into his bedroom to catch a few hours sleep before his shift. Maggie didn't mind the solitude in the least, and felt more than comfortable being left to her own devices.

Although she understood their concern, she still resented Cale and his brothers talking her into spending the night with their aunt. But when the Perry brothers turned on the charm, even the most cold-hearted woman would be hard-pressed to deny them whatever they wanted.

She genuinely liked Cale's brothers. They were good men and they shared a bond she could never hope to understand, which led her to believe she must be an only child.

She liberated Cale's laptop computer from the rolltop desk in the living room, then settled down in the cozy morning room with a can of cola and the Saturday edition of the *LA Times*. A soft sea breeze occasionally caused the miniblinds to slap against the window frame while Gilda played quietly with a colorful ladder in her cage. Pearl napped on the floor beneath the table at Maggie's feet. Even the cats had decided to join her, stretching out on the small wicker buffet table beneath the rays of sunlight filtering into the room. She'd never feel lonely with such a menagerie for company.

While she waited for the computer to boot up, she opened the newspaper and immediately located the obituaries. She scanned the names and photos until one caught her attention. Britta Fenway, a thirty-two-year-old single woman whose life had ended tragically in a boating accident off Catalina Island. Without considering why, Maggie circled the name with the black felt-tipped pen she'd snagged from Cale's drawer.

She set the newspaper aside and turned her attention to the computer, her intent to make a list of the fragmented pieces of the dreams and images she'd been recalling, hoping that by putting them into words, she might find a pattern to her thoughts. She had her doubts the wispy images would actually lead her to more solid clues about herself, but at least if she put them down into some semblance of order, she could attempt to view them objectively. If luck were on her side for a change, she might even garner a few clues to lead her to someone who knew she existed. Perhaps even the man hidden in the shadows of her dreams.

She called up the word processing program and started jotting notes as they came to her. The cast made her typing skills feel elementary at best, yet, despite the cumbersome hindrance, her fingers fell easily over the correct keys. The three pages of notes were as scattered and disconnected as her dreams, but the progress pleased her. She saved the file to print later, then called up another blank sheet. How she knew her way around the word processing program she really couldn't guess, but there was no denying how naturally it came to her.

Feeling truly hopeful for the first time in days, she started typing again, noting the various physical items from her dreams. Halfway through the list, her mind wandered back to the man hidden in the shadows. Who was he? He meant a great deal to her, that much she did know. A relative, perhaps? Or possibly a mentor? She couldn't say with absolute certainty, but she had a strong feeling that whoever he was, there was nothing romantic about their liaison.

She pulled in a deep, relaxing breath, sat back then closed her eyes. After two more deep cleansing breaths, the first image came to her. With her eyes still closed, she sat up and settled her fingers over the keyboard. She typed, sporadically at first, as the images floated in and out of her consciousness.

She took down the bits and pieces of conversation she heard from people who were unfamiliar to her. She documented the time and space of places she couldn't remember ever visiting. A range of emotions, too many to capture in a single thought, swamped her and clamored for attention. Her only hope of understanding them was to record them for later dissection.

Then she saw him. A wall of glass separated them,

but she saw him clearly. Fear for his safety climbed her spine. He shouldn't have come.

A hand touched her shoulder. It was time to go.

She stood to leave. Sadness cloaked him, the emotion palpable in his dark chocolate-colored eyes as he looked at her and mouthed an apology she couldn't hear. The lines of his face were deeper than usual. The gray at his temples, which had always given him a distinguished quality, were whiter than she remembered.

For the first time in her life, her father looked every second of his fifty-eight years.

AFTERNOON SHADOWS darkened the bedroom as Cale slowly opened his eyes. He turned his head on the pillow to check the bedside clock in case he'd either inadvertently failed to set the alarm or had hit the snooze button in his sleep, the latter being the most likely. Rising, he glanced around the room, a little surprised to find himself alone since he could always count on Frankie and Johnny for company when an afternoon nap was involved.

After a quick steaming shower to help shed the last vestiges of sleep, he dressed and went in search of Maggie. Since she'd already packed what she needed for girls' night at Deb's into the small nylon duffel he'd loaned her, they had plenty of time for an early supper out if they left within the next twenty minutes or so. That way they wouldn't have to rush, and he'd still have plenty of time to drop her off and make it to the station house before his shift began.

The living room was empty. He turned, about to

head downstairs to check the guestroom, but stopped and listened. A repetitive, rhythmic clicking sound drifted toward him. He concentrated, quickly determining the noise was coming from the morning room.

He turned back and walked through the kitchen to the morning room. There, seated at the table with his laptop, sat Maggie, typing with record speed. Given the cumbersome cast, he was more than impressed by the constant rhythmic click of the keys as her fingers literally flew over the keyboard.

He gently cleared his throat, not wanting to startle her. She didn't so much as flinch, just kept typing away, her sole focus the laptop's monitor. Pearl did react, however, her tail thumping against the tiled floor in greeting.

Impervious to the intrusion, Maggie continued typing. Pearl slowly stretched. With her big paws in front of her, she lifted her rump in the air and issued a dramatic groan before straightening lazily. Pearl nudged Maggie's leg with her muzzle as if signaling they had company, then made her way out from beneath the table.

Maggie let out a contented sigh. Her hands fell from the keyboard and she leaned back in the chair, a satisfied expression on her beautiful face. She must have sensed his presence, because she turned her head in his direction.

The smile curving her luscious mouth was bright enough to lighten the room. "How long have you been standing there?"

"Not long." He pulled out a chair and sat. "What have you been up to?"

She leaned forward and entered a few commands in the computer. "I had a breakthrough."

Had she recovered the missing pieces of her past? His heart thumped behind his ribs, whether from excitement or dread, he couldn't be sure. "What kind of breakthrough?" he asked cautiously.

She closed the lid of the laptop with a snap, then flashed him another one of those high-wattage smiles. "I work for sex."

# 9

"SEX," Cale muttered, for what had to be the fiftieth time in the last three hours. If there was one thing he could say about Maggie, it was that she certainly kept him on his toes. God only knew what she'd reveal to him next.

He returned the portable defibrillator to its storage place behind the side panel of the ambulance. He was still recovering from the initial shock of Maggie's outrageous statement. Once she'd stopped laughing at his misconception, she'd explained that she didn't work for "sex," but for S.E.C.S., which she thought was a governmental agency of some kind.

Before he'd had time to digest that wild explanation, she'd delivered the news that she'd "seen" her father, although she couldn't fully explain where she'd been at the time. The details she'd been intent on discussing over dinner were sketchy at best, which did nothing to ease her frustration, or reduce the nagging suspicion in the back of his mind.

He should be happy for her. She was making progress, and that was a good thing.

Wasn't it?

"Woman trouble already?"

Cale snapped the right side panel of the rig closed

and turned to find Scorch walking toward him. "What makes you say that?"

Scorch leaned his shoulder against the rig. "Because I recognize the look." He kept his voice low. "It's the same one I've been seeing in the mirror lately."

Beneath the bright fluorescent glare of the overhead lights in the bay, Cale stared hard at his friend. "Yeah? And what look is that?"

Scorch glanced quickly around the deserted area, then back at Cale. "The one that tells the whole friggin' world there's a woman who's got you tied up in knots, man."

No matter how much he wished otherwise, Cale didn't have the heart to disagree with Scorch. How could he when his temporary partner for the night had nailed exactly how he'd been feeling since Maggie blindsided him with her most recent revelation? Each memory she recalled baffled him even more and made him feel as if she was slipping away from him. Not that she'd ever been his in the first place, he reminded himself.

"Well?" Scorch prompted. "Has Amnesia Chick got you all twisted, or what?"

Cale walked around to the back of the rig and opened the door. "Her name is Maggie," he said, his tone sharper than he'd intended. "And there's nothing to get all twisted about. Once her memory returns, she'll be moving on."

That's why he was in a bad mood, he realized. Each memory Maggie recovered brought her closer to saying goodbye. He couldn't explain why it bothered him. Once he'd served their purpose, didn't they always walk away in the end? Why should Maggie be different?

Because she'd gotten under his skin, that's why. Because he couldn't get through an hour without thinking about her. Because, dammit, he didn't want her to leave once her issues were resolved.

Scorch followed him and stood outside the open door of the rig. "Then what are you getting all defensive about? Unless…"

*Unless this one means more to you,* Cale finished silently and frowned.

He shoved the thought aside and checked each of the drawers and cabinets, making sure they had ample supplies for the night ahead. He'd worked enough Saturday nights to know the current lull wouldn't last for long.

"Unless you help me take a quick inventory before we get a call," he said to Scorch, "we could be in it deep. The bars and dance clubs will be closing in about six hours."

Scorch rubbed at the back of his neck with his hand, then climbed into the rig with Cale. "Women can be a pain," he muttered.

Cale stopped his count of the gauze pads. "Any woman in particular?" Maybe if he focused on Scorch's problems instead of his own, his mood would improve. Not likely, but worth a shot.

Scorch nodded and looked away. "An E.R. nurse."

"Which one?"

"Tilly. And don't go getting all big brother on me,

either," Scorch warned. "This is serious, so keep it to yourself for a while."

Cale appreciated Scorch's reluctance to publicly announce his interest in Tilly since the guys in the house had a reputation as world-class pranksters that respected little in the way of boundaries.

"You ask her out yet?"

"Twice," Scorch admitted. "She turned me down flat, too."

"Maybe she's not interested."

Scorch finger-combed his spiky red hair and thought quietly for a moment. "Nah. A stud like me? She'll be putty in my hands."

The self-proclaimed stud was about as scrawny as a sixteen-year-old. Still, Tom "Scorch" McDonough rarely came stag to any of the functions the guys hosted, which had to account for something about his appeal to the opposite sex.

Cale laughed. "Uh-huh. That explains why she's rejected you. Twice."

Half an hour later, the inventory and restocking complete, Cale closed up the rig and walked out of the bay. Scorch followed, and together they stood quietly absorbing the hushed sounds of the city as dusk settled over Santa Monica. Cale stuffed his hands in the front pockets of his uniform trousers and looked up at the darkening sky.

Maggie's words drifted into his consciousness.

*A wall of glass separated us.*

"What kind of places do you know of that could have a wall of glass in them?"

"Hospitals," Scorch suggested with a shrug. "Why do you ask?"

Cale thought of the E.R., then shook his head. "No particular reason," he said, knowing his friend would respect his willingness to keep certain information to himself. "What about a bank?"

*Someone touched my shoulder, as if my time was up.*

The peaceful night sounds of the city surrounded them. Cale understood, as did all the guys who worked the night shift, that before much longer there'd be nothing peaceful about a city quite often filled with random violence and tragedy. L.A. was still a great place, and Cale couldn't imagine living anywhere else. There weren't many areas that could lay claim to stretches of sandy beaches, awe-inspiring mountain ranges or the wide expanse and beauty of the desert, not to mention just about any form of entertainment. In his line of work, however, he tended to experience more of its less-than-stellar characteristics.

"Banks usually have an open-floor plan," Scorch answered after a few minutes. "What about a visiting area?"

*He said he was sorry, but I couldn't hear his voice because of the glass separating us.*

A dead weight landed on Cale's chest. "A visiting area?" He hoped like hell the conclusion he'd just drawn had taken a wrong turn.

"Sure," Scorch said. "You know, like at a prison."

Cale let out a long, slow breath. "Yeah," he said solemnly. "That's what I was thinking, too."

"IT'S A PROVEN medical fact that chocolate is good for you." To prove her point, Tilly snatched another piece of Debbie's homemade fudge from the square tin before passing it around to Maggie. "I'm a nurse, I know about these things."

Maggie filched another piece of the creamy-smooth candy and bit into it. Rich flavor exploded in her mouth. She briefly closed her eyes and moaned in ecstasy. The word *willpower* had obviously been deleted from her vocabulary, but when chocolate was involved, especially homemade, who cared?

She opened her eyes and passed the tin to Cale's aunt.

"Of course, it is," Debbie added, her soft blue eyes twinkling with mischief. "Done right, chocolate will cover at least a few of the basic food groups—fruit, dairy and grains."

Maggie downed the last of her second margarita for the night. Her reluctance to stay with Cale's aunt had dissipated less than five minutes after she'd arrived. Debbie Perry was a warm, kind woman with laughing eyes and a quick smile. It was easy to see where Cale and his brothers had obtained their senses of humor.

Maggie lifted her empty glass. "Chocolate is a vegetable," she proclaimed regally.

Tilly's gentle laughter filled the room. "A veggie?" She slipped a strand of her chin-length sable hair behind her ear. "Fat, yes, but come on, Maggie. Veggie is pushing it, don't you think?"

"There is no fat whatsoever in chocolate, ladies,"

Debbie reminded them with mock sternness. "And don't either of you dare to burst my bubble, either."

She took their empty glasses and headed toward the kitchen. Within seconds the sound of the blender echoed through the open area into the family room.

"Sure," Maggie said, grateful Debbie went heavy on the strawberry margarita mix and easy on the tequila. "Chocolate comes from cocoa beans, right? Beans are a vegetable, so it qualifies."

"That's a thin one." Tilly said loud enough to be heard over the blender. "And that only covers one food group."

The blender stopped and Debbie refilled their glasses. "Chocolate cake," she said, signaling to them that drinks were served. "Grain."

Maggie stood, hitched up the loose-fitting pajama bottoms she wore and giggled. "*Milk* chocolate."

"Chocolate-covered cherries," Debbie added. "And chocolate-covered raisins."

Tilly took the glass Debbie offered and handed it to Maggie. "Ooh," Tilly said, "strawberries dipped in chocolate."

Maggie wondered if Cale liked strawberries. "Hmm, with champagne," she added. Would Cale like strawberries and champagne...in bed?

"For two," Tilly added, then walked slowly back into the family room to the big comfy L-shaped sofa.

Maggie and Debbie followed. Feeling slightly light-headed, Maggie took extra care with her steps. So far, all Drew had been right about as far as an evening spent with Debbie and Tilly was the chocolate.

The girl talk, pajamas and strawberry margaritas had been a welcome and liberating surprise.

"Anyone special in mind?" Debbie asked Tilly, settling back on the sofa.

A slow smile curved Tilly's lips. "Maybe."

Maggie sat in the corner section of the sofa and curled her feet beneath her. "Does he know?" she asked curiously. She herself was attracted to Cale, and she suspected the feeling was mutual, but she couldn't say with exact certainty. Although, she thought, hiding a smile behind her glass, the odds were stacked in her favor after her outrageous behavior this morning. He'd looked so pained, she'd almost taken pity on him. Maybe she would have, if she hadn't been suffering, as well.

"He should." Tilly took a sip of her drink. "He's been flirting with me for weeks."

"Has he asked you out?" Maggie asked.

"A couple of times."

Debbie set her glass on the table. She reached for the tin of fudge and hesitated, then snagged another piece for herself. "And you haven't said yes?"

Tilly wrinkled her pert nose. "I don't know." She turned to rest her back against the big square pillow propped on the arm of the sofa, then sat cross-legged. "I'm not sure if I want to get involved in another relationship right now."

"Tilly Jensen," Debbie scolded. "It's been over a year since you broke up with what's-his-name. You should be more than ready."

"*Ready* isn't exactly my problem."

Maggie took a sip of her drink and silently agreed.

Her problems were vast, but being ready definitely was not one of them. When she wasn't worrying about who or what she was, all she could think about was Cale. Since her little stunt this morning, making love to him was easily the most prominent thought.

She let out a little sigh of pleasure. The fantasies were endless.

Debbie adjusted her long, sapphire silk robe over her legs. "I meant for a relationship."

"Why can't it just be about sex?"

Maggie agreed with Tilly. "Really," she added. "Guys do it all the time."

Could she make love to Cale and keep her heart out of the equation? Probably not, since she had her doubts about being the love 'em and leave 'em type.

"Exactly my point," Tilly said. "If they can have sex without all the hearts and flowers, then why is it still a crime if we do? 'You've come a long way, baby,' my ass."

"I suppose if that's the kind of relationship you really want," Debbie's expression turned thoughtful.

"Uh-oh, she used 'the tone.'" Tilly's laughter held the slightest hint of caution. "Get ready, Maggie. Here it comes."

Debbie waved her hand in dismissal at Tilly. "You're going to frighten Maggie away."

Feeling decidedly woozy, Maggie set her drink on the table. "I don't think I scare that easily."

"Boy, I'll say," Tilly agreed. "Drew told me she put Ben in his place this morning *and* earned his respect. That's not an easy accomplishment."

Debbie gave Tilly a stern look. "You're changing the subject."

"Okay. Fine." Tilly raised her hands in surrender. "Lecture away."

"I'm not going to lecture you. I was only going to suggest that after a while, sexual attraction fades."

"Isn't that the point? And for the record, it hasn't hurt Drew any."

Debbie looked at Maggie and smiled. "Drew's really very lonely."

As fascinating as Maggie found the subject, Cale was the one who interested her. She wanted to know everything about him. His likes. His dislikes. What it'd be like to make love to him, she thought again.

"As if." Tilly's laughter deepened. "With all the women he has falling at his feet? That man doesn't have time be lonely."

"You two are very close, aren't you?" Maggie asked in an effort to derail her fantasies of Cale before they started up again.

*As if,* she thought and stifled a giggle.

Tilly nodded. "Ever since we were kids, and I beat him up for running over my dolls with his bike. I think we were around seven or eight years old at the time."

"They've been inseparable ever since," Debbie added.

"Have you and he ever...?"

"Oh, good grief, no." A mock shiver shook Tilly's thin frame and she giggled. "I did have a crush on Ben, though, when I was in the seventh grade. He thought I was a pest.'' She took a sip of her drink, then giggled again. ''He still thinks I'm a pest.''

''That's because to him, you're the sister he never had.'' To Maggie, Debbie said, ''All three boys were always looking out for Tilly.''

The impression of loneliness Maggie had experienced during breakfast with Cale and his brothers returned. Her free-association exercise this afternoon had led her to believe that she did in fact have at least a semblance of a family, somewhere. In particular, a father. But for reasons she couldn't quite explain, the man in her vision didn't seem completely real to her. Although she remembered him, she couldn't exactly say she *knew* him.

There, she realized suddenly, stood the cause for the loneliness and longing that continued to cloak her. She felt a lack of belonging. Cale and his brothers. Their aunt. Even Tilly, whose status was merely that of a longtime family friend, they all *belonged*. Maggie didn't think she'd experienced the true sense of family, of being a part of a greater whole, in a very long time.

Tilly pulled her knees up to her chest and wrapped her arms around them. ''Do you know how many dates I didn't have because of the Perry brothers? Drew and I were at the Farmer's Market a couple of weeks ago and ran into Neal Turner. The poor guy's still afraid to speak to me.''

Debbie shook her head. ''I don't remember him.''

''You should. In high school Cale got a two-day suspension for clocking him one in the jaw.'' Tilly turned to Maggie. ''They were in the boys locker room when Cale overheard Neal bragging to a couple of his buddies that once he got what he wanted, he was dumping me."

"Oh, my," Maggie murmured, although she really wasn't all that surprised, the man had a protective streak wider than the Grand Canyon.

"Do you know how hard it is to get a date for the prom when half the guys in high school are terrified of being pulverized if they make one wrong move?"

"Cale took you to your prom," Debbie reminded her gently.

Tilly issued a short burst of laughter. "Out of guilt. It was his fault no one else asked me."

That sounded like the Cale she knew, Maggie thought. "Has he always been so..."

"Protective?" Tilly supplied.

Maggie nodded.

"For as long as I've known him," Tilly said. "He collected more strays than the local animal shelter, the humane society eventually put him on their rescue list. Isn't he still a member?"

Debbie nodded. "I never knew what he was going to bring home next," she said. "At one point we received a warning from animal control because Cale had too many animals."

"We still think it was the nosey old biddy who used to live across the street that turned him in," Tilly added. "She hated just about everyone in the neighborhood. My dad let Cale keep a few of his pets in our backyard until he found homes for them."

"Your poor father." Debbie chuckled softly at the

memory. "He had no idea how much of an ordeal that would turn into, did he?"

Tilly's brown eyes filled with affection. "The goose just didn't like Dad."

Maggie's heart gave a sharp tug. She couldn't help wondering if she was just one more stray in need of saving in Cale's mind. "He hasn't changed much, has he?"

"No," Debbie answered. "Not really. No one was surprised when he decided to become a paramedic. He's been saving people and animals since my brother passed away."

Maggie thought of the image of her father. The only emotion she could honestly attach to the memory was a strong sense of curiosity to know more about him. "That must've been so difficult for all of them," she said.

"Losing both of their parents, especially when they were all so young... Well," Debbie said, "it's bound to have an effect. I see it, even if they can't, or won't."

"Oh, absolutely." Tilly agreed solemnly. "Drew won't let any woman get too close. Cale still thinks it's his job to save the world. And I've never been able to figure out what makes Ben tick."

Maggie wanted to know what made Cale tick. His collection of strays, his reasons for becoming a paramedic all made sense to her on a psychological level. By saving those around him, he subconsciously fulfilled some childhood fantasy. The effect wasn't exactly what she'd call adverse because he was kind, generous and possessed a deep caring nature. Still, she'd begun to sense he held back a part of himself.

She didn't believe him to be in the emotionally bankrupt league, scorned by a woman or crippled by his past, but something lurked in his psyche that prevented him from truly giving all of himself.

Debbie leaned forward to cover the half-empty tin of chocolate. "Ben's more complex," she offered by way of explanation to Maggie. "He keeps things to himself more than the other two. After Joanna died, Alex, my brother, stopped caring about everything. Ben took on a lot for a kid his age."

"Do you mind if I ask how their mother died?"

"In a fire," Debbie said quietly. "She was one of the first women firefighters in the state, and quite proud of the fact. Joanna and Alex worked in separate fire stations, and usually different shifts for the most part, but occasionally they'd have a scheduling conflict so I'd watch the boys for them.

"A fire started one night in the garment district. Joanna and her team were one of the first on the scene, but by the time they'd arrived, the fire had already began to spread to the neighboring buildings. Engine crews from all over the county were called in to assist, Alex's being one of them."

Sadness engulfed Debbie's soft blue eyes. "The fire moved to what was supposed to be an abandoned building, but the team found out some transients were trapped on one of the upper floors. Joanna went in with three other firefighters.

"She did manage to save them, but something went wrong. The ceiling collapsed and trapped her. Alex tried to save her, but by the time he was able to reach her, it was too late. She'd not only suffered from smoke inhalation because her helmet had been knocked loose, but her burns were extensive. All the doctors could do for her was make her as comfortable as possible.''

Maggie's heart broke for the young boys who'd lost their mother so tragically.

Debbie rose from the sofa and walked over to the stereo to add more CDs to the changer. ''My brother never got over losing Joanna,'' she continued, resuming her seat. ''He really did try at first for the sake of the boys, but he'd lost his heart in that fire. He had nothing left to give them. He was only thirty-eight when he died of a massive coronary less than two years later.''

An image flashed in Maggie's mind, then vanished before she could fully grasp it, leaving behind pain that reached deep into her soul.

Was what she experienced for Cale, she wondered, and the loss he and his brothers had suffered? Or was it much more personal?

She downed her margarita, saddened by the knowledge she might never know the answer.

# 10

"A JOB? You're serious?"

Cale flinched at Maggie's squeal of delight, then winced when hot coffee unexpectedly singed the tip of his tongue.

He stifled a curse. What was his aunt thinking, offering Maggie a job? Didn't she realize Maggie could very well be what she'd been trying to tell him all along—a criminal? Or, at the very least, an ex-con?

All night, during his shift, he'd wrestled with the conclusion he'd drawn. Questioning Maggie about the memory she'd had of her father would be a useless endeavor because he already knew from experience that her powers of recollection were limited. He'd tried several times to arrive at another less-incriminating explanation for her dream that made sense, but he always came back to the same conclusion. Maggie LaRue, which might not be her real name, was quite likely a jailbird.

Debbie handed him a paper towel to wipe up the mess he'd made on the breakfast bar. "You bet I am," she said brightly to Maggie.

"But..." *But she might be a criminal!* Cale wanted to say.

One look at the sheer delight on Maggie's sweet

face and the words died on his lips. No matter what conclusions he'd drawn about her, he simply didn't have the heart to trample her happiness over something as simple as a job in a bookstore. "Can you legally employ her when she doesn't have a social security number?" he asked lamely.

Debbie stood and gave his shoulder a reassuring pat before clearing away the last of the breakfast dishes. "Don't you worry about it. It's only part-time temporary, and I really could use some extra help around the store a couple days a week for a while."

Not willing to give up the fight too quickly, he asked Maggie, "Won't it be a little much for you? You're supposed to rest."

"Nonsense," Debbie answered before Maggie had the chance to respond. "It'll keep her mind occupied on something other than her problems."

Maggie flashed him one of her irresistible smiles. "I want to, Cale. It really could help me if I have something else to keep my mind busy."

"It's settled then," Debbie proclaimed before he could issue another protest. "You can start tomorrow. I'll pick you up about nine-thirty."

Maggie pushed her bar stool back and stood, holding on to the waistband of her blue pajama bottoms. "I can't thank you enough for this, Debbie." She hesitated, her eyes filling with uncertainty for a moment before she wrapped her slender arms around Cale's aunt for a brief hug.

The minute she let go of the waistband, the pajama bottoms drooped, slinging low on the curve of her hips. The matching cami inched upward, revealing yards of luscious skin. Cale stared, appreciating the view more than was wise.

"And, you," She turned to face him, her eyes still sparkling with sheer happiness. "I'll be able to start repaying you for all you've done for me."

He waved away her offer, not trusting himself to keep his opinions to himself. Emotions crowded him, making him edgy. Concern for his aunt that Maggie could very well be the criminal she feared herself to be. Worry that Maggie would do too much when she was supposed to take it easy, thereby slowing her recovery. Confusion over his own inability to completely reconcile the sketchy facts they were both learning about her past with the woman who charmed his family and insisted on repaying him for a few clothing items.

Lust wasn't the only emotion ranking high on his list of concerns. He'd be a liar if he denied his attraction to Maggie, or that she was slowly coming to mean more to him than just another woman in need.

Keeping his distance would be the smart thing to do. Too bad he was feeling a whole lot like the village idiot.

*Time to face facts, pal. Maggie is a walking, talking paradox you might never fully understand.*

Oh, but the enjoyment of unraveling all those secrets was way too tempting.

"I won't be long," Maggie said. Her gaze still held a light-heartedness destined to give his conscience a sharp jolt and fill him with guilt.

He let out a resigned sigh and took a sip of his coffee while his aunt explained to Maggie where to find the towels, as well as how to use the temperamental taps of the shower. He made a mental note to call a plumber for his aunt first thing Monday morning.

The crossword puzzle from the Sunday paper sat on the bar. It mocked him. Just as the memory of Maggie's kiss-swollen lips taunted him with that three-letter word for aroused.

After Maggie disappeared upstairs, Debbie poured herself another cup of coffee then climbed onto the bar stool across from him. "You got something on your mind, Cale?"

Did he ever. His thoughts were scattered and made about as much sense as Maggie's faulty long-term memory. He set the mug in front of him and wrapped his hands around the warm ceramic. "You don't know anything about her," he said, "and you're giving her a job."

Debbie lifted a pale blond eyebrow. "Neither do you," she reminded him. "And she's living with you."

"She's not living with me. I've just offered her a place to stay. It's not the same thing."

The knowing smile and patient expression on his aunt's face told him loud and clear she saw straight through his flimsy argument.

He looked away and stared into his coffee, warring with the decision to enlighten Debbie of the inconceivable, yet possibly true, details surrounding Maggie. For the briefest of instants, he almost wished he could be more like his brothers. Especially Drew. With his blithe approach to women, he wouldn't give a rip what dark secrets lurked in Maggie's past. Come what may, he'd be damned sure they both reveled in plenty of sensual delights during the time they did have together.

Cale wasn't at all like Ben, either, he realized. Ben never would've gotten himself in this position in the first place. Ben might have offered his assistance to Maggie in a much less involving manner, and he never would have brought her into his life the way Cale had done.

"What is it, honey?" Debbie asked him quietly.

He looked back at his aunt, who he loved with all his heart. Debbie was the only mother he'd known since he was just a kid. She hadn't even been the age he was now when she'd assumed sole responsibility for her nephews, and never once in all the years spent raising them could he remember her ever putting her needs and wants before their own.

"There's something you should know about Maggie," he said. His aunt listened while he explained about the fragmented dreams, visions or memories Maggie continued to recall little by little. He told her about the break-and-enter trick she'd pulled, the incident on the beach, and finally the likelihood that she had a criminal history.

When he finished, Debbie remained quiet and thoughtful. He searched her gaze and nearly groaned aloud with dread. She had that look, the one that said she knew the answer but it was up to him to figure it out for himself. He'd seen it enough times growing up, especially when it came to his English homework. He took a long drink of his coffee and braced himself.

"Ask her about it," she suggested.

He shook his head. "I can't. No pressure, remember?"

She reached across the breakfast bar and took his hands with hers, her touch as warm and gentle as ever. "What is your heart telling you?"

"What do you mean?" A stall tactic if he'd ever heard one.

She saw right through him. Again. "Tell me your impressions of the woman who's *staying* with you."

He chuckled, then leaned against the back of the bar stool and crossed his arms over his chest. "Sweet. Intelligent. Caring," he answered with ease. "The animals love her. Since she's been there, Pearl's practically deserted me."

"You know what they say about animals being good judges of character," Debbie said, as if he needed reminding.

"She's funny. Frustratingly independent. And confusing as hell." He failed to mention sexy as sin, a thought he had the wisdom to keep to himself.

"Your brothers certainly like her, and Tilly and I had a wonderful time with her last night." Debbie gave her head a slight shake, her graying hair swaying with the movement. "No, Cale. I'm sorry, but what you're saying about her alleged past does not coincide with that adorable young woman. You saw her. She was ecstatic over measly part-time employment. Does that sound at all like a woman who's led a nefarious lifestyle?"

"No. It doesn't," he admitted with a sigh. He wasn't sure whether he was supposed to feel better or not. He certainly was no less confused. "Any suggestions?"

"Time." Debbie slid off the bar stool and came to his side, circling her arms affectionately around his shoulders. "And, honey?"

He didn't need to look up to know her expression would be filled with love and affection. "Yeah?"

"Trust your heart. The heart never lies."

DISCOURAGED, although not completely disheartened by her lack of progress, Maggie gave up and shut down the laptop for the time being. She'd spent a little over three uninterrupted hours in front of the computer and hadn't been granted so much as a glimmer of insight into her past for her trouble.

Her Internet search for S.E.C.S. had turned up nothing. Of all the search engines she'd attempted, each had directed her to the Securities and Exchange Commission, which she promptly eliminated as a possibility when she drew an absolute blank as far as a connection in her sorry excuse for a memory.

The online white pages had been equally futile. No listings for M. LaRue, Maggie LaRue or Margaret LaRue came up in any of the major metropolitan areas she'd searched. The one possible lead she'd encountered in the Atlanta white pages fell apart upon further research when she'd discovered an M.E. LaRue was a twenty-two year old male.

Not that she'd expected to actually find a listing for herself. She couldn't even state with absolute certainty that Maggie LaRue even existed, let alone be fortunate enough to locate an obituary under that name. Maybe she hadn't gotten the name off a head-stone after all.

She slipped a loose strand of hair behind her ear. Until she remembered her actual, *legal* identity, she wasn't about to hold her breath. She had a better chance of turning purple before she managed to un-earth the truth at this point.

At least the online medical Web sites she'd visited for information regarding her condition had offered a tad more by way of useful data. According to the ar-ticles she'd read on level III amnesia, the accident it-self might forever be erased from her mind, but her chances were better than mediocre for the return of most, if not all, of her long-term memory. A down-side did exist, however, in that it could take literally years for a full recovery.

She sighed and rolled her shoulders to ease the stiffness. The pages of notes she'd typed the day be-fore lay next to the computer. She slid them from the oak rolltop desk and read through them again. She'd given another go at free-association when she'd first turned on the computer, but all she'd gotten for her trouble had been a blinking cursor atop a blank page.

A slow smile tugged her lips. Well, she had man-aged some serious daydreaming...with Cale cast in the starring role.

With a brisk shake of her head, she temporarily squelched the fantasies before they could resurface. She forced herself to concentrate on her notes, but they might as well have been a work of fiction for as much as they nudged her faulty gray matter.

Realizing her limit, she pushed away from the desk

and stood, stretching to work out the kinks from sitting hunched over the computer for so long. The novels Debbie had given her to read to help pass the time still sat on the coffee table where Maggie had left them this morning. She briefly considered taking one with her out to the patio, but her mood called for more of a physical activity.

"Come on, Pearl," she called to the dog who'd been snoring softly from her big stuffed pillow in the corner of the living room. "Maybe some fresh air will help."

Pearl barely opened her dark, almond-shaped eyes long enough to lift her head from her paws, before she flopped over onto her side and closed them again.

Maggie laughed softly. "Okay, I'll do my own fresh air."

She had serious doubts something as innocuous as a breath or two of warm, sea-scented air would offer much assistance in breaking down the barriers surrounding her memories. What she really needed was a distraction, physical activity that required little thought. Maybe she'd raid the garage for gardening tools and unearth the weeds choking the planters in the front of the house.

Now she *was* getting desperate, she thought, if the idea of digging in the dirt appealed to her. Worse still, she compounded the desperate thought by trying to figure out how to wrap up her cast to protect it from the dirt.

Desperation did strange things to a person, she thought as she went searching for Cale. There was no sign of him in the kitchen or the breakfast area, so she tried his bedroom. The door stood wide open, so she peeked inside only to find it perfectly neat and deserted.

Her gaze zeroed in on the bed. "No," she said firmly. "Do *not* go there."

She practically scurried down the hallway to the staircase, then hurried downstairs in record time. "Cale?"

No answer.

She crossed to the sliding glass doors and opened the screen. "Cale?" she called again, but the backyard was deserted, as well.

Shielding her eyes, she walked outside to the edge of the patio and looked upward to the midafternoon sun riding high and warm in the cloudless sky. A gentle breeze carried the salty scent of the ocean, and pulled a few wisps of hair free from the haphazard knot she'd loosely secured on top of her head with a pencil.

"Any luck?"

Maggie turned at the sound of Cale's deep voice. He stood in the open doorway, his hands braced over his head. He used the tips of his fingers for support on the top ledge of the track, leaning slightly forward.

Now, there existed a sight more than worthy of the term *distraction*.

"I was looking for you." She hadn't meant her voice to go all low and sultry, but from the quick flash of desire lighting his eyes, she wasn't about to start complaining.

An easy, sinful smile curved his mouth. "You found me."

Regardless of her lack of memory, she didn't think for a minute she'd ever been subjected to such blatant male sensuality. That sexy little grin. The hint of mischief, combined with heated desire in his eyes. A body worthy of a Bernini sculpture. Cale Perry was, hands-down, the ultimate fantasy in the flesh.

She took her sweet time, treasuring every second of her leisurely perusal of all that male perfection. The plain white T-shirt tucked into a pair of faded jeans clung to his body, outlining the width of his chest. Rather than allowing her imagination free rein, she craved to feel the smooth, sleek skin beneath the cotton fabric clinging to him for herself. To take her time and fully explore each hill and valley of the exotic landscape of his body.

The snug sleeves emphasized his thick, muscled biceps, effectively drawing her gaze to the corded strength beneath the tanned flesh of his forearms. The urge to intimately acquaint herself with all that power and sinew shook her. Hard. So hard, breathing suddenly took a concentrated effort.

"Maggie?"

Reluctantly, she dragged her gaze back to his face. "Yes?"

That killer grin deepened. "Did you need something?"

"Need?" she parroted. She had plenty, and wondered what his reaction would be if she told him exactly what type of *need* occupied her mind. The kind that practically guaranteed sweeping them away, carrying them where mutual pleasure awaited, catapulting them into a place just shy of heaven. Into paradise.

He balanced himself as his arms fell to his sides. Slowly, he walked barefoot through the open doorway. His hypnotic gaze remained locked with hers, drawing her deeper under his erotic spell. "You said you were looking for me."

Her vocal chords refused to function, so she nodded lamely. Yes, why *had* she been looking for him? she wondered, hardly surprised when no coherent reply immediately sprang to mind. Surely, he didn't expect her to think straight when her hormones were zinging off the charts.

Two more perfectly measured steps and he stopped. Mere inches separated them. He crowded her, invaded her space and shook the last of her dormant feminine senses from their dazed slumber. Her instincts screamed at her to retreat, but not a single argument existed in her mind as to why she should pay attention to such a ludicrous demand, especially not with her body already humming in acute awareness.

Her past, her identity, even her future remained a mystery. The present, however, was suddenly as clear as the blue, cloudless sky overhead. One touch. One whispered word. One sensually demanding kiss and at least one of the mysteries haunting her would be solved—she'd no longer have to wonder what it would be like to make love to Cale.

She was no frail and delicate female ready to wilt when faced by the pure, unadulterated sensuality of a sexually appealing male. Nor was she willing to wait around for him to take the decision out of her hands. She wanted Cale, which was probably the most truthful statement about herself right now. That and a willingness to live for the moment, to stop stressing over what had come before in her life or the unknowns that remained ahead. Once her memory surfaced, she imagined her life would lead her elsewhere. Why shouldn't she live for the moment, when the present was all that truly belonged to her?

"Yes." She cleared her throat. "Yes," she said with more force. "I do need something."

Hesitation flared briefly in his gaze. Would he deny her?

"What is it, Maggie?" he asked, his voice as rich and smooth as the finest Kentucky bourbon. "What do you need?"

She lifted her good hand and gently placed it on his chest, near the vicinity of his heart. The strong, sure rhythm beat in rapid cadence against her palm, reassuring her he shared the same need, the same desire, the same deep wanting that was consuming her.

The remaining distance evaporated as she inched closer, then reached up to brush her lips lightly over his. "You," she whispered softly. "I need you, Cale."

# 11

CALE WANTED nothing more than to fulfill Maggie's sensual request. His body all but demanded he comply and he'd willingly give his left arm if it meant spending the rest of the day tangled in the sheets with her. Already his Levi's felt as if they'd shrunk two sizes.

He struggled hard to resist the need clamoring inside him. From the sultry heat simmering in Maggie's eyes to the featherlight brush of her mouth against his, his chance of winning the battle was nada. *Hypocrite* was the last label anyone could ever slap him with...until now.

How could he possibly make love to her? Her existence remained in a constant state of chaotic turmoil. Snippets of memories that barely made sense on their own were a thousand times more bewildering if he added them all together. One and one might equal two, but where Maggie was concerned, the equation might as well add up to eight-thousand, nine-hundred and twenty-seven for as much sense as her disjointed recollections meant. Did he really want the responsibility of compounding her problems with the issues making love to her might raise?

Sure he could, he thought, if sex was his only interest. If he didn't give a rip what happened to Maggie, he wouldn't give a second thought about lifting her into his arms and carrying her to the closest bed. Except, he did care. He always cared.

Her palm pressed against his heart, her touch heating his skin though the thin material of the cotton T-shirt. He was his own worst enemy, he realized. Not a single one of his noble intentions stood a chance of survival against the bewitching woman asking him to make love to her.

With more reluctance than he dreamed possible, he slipped his hand over hers and carefully removed her palm from his chest. "Maggie…"

"Uh-uh," she said, a frown marring her perfect peaches-and-cream complexion. The pencil loosely securing her hair clattered to the ground as she shook her head, freeing all those lush strands so they fell down her back in soft, gentle waves. "Please don't tell me I've just misread the signs."

The warm breeze tossed wisps of red hair across her face. His hands itched to rub it between his fingers and feel the satiny texture against his skin. He imagined her hair draped across his stomach, feeling the silken glide of her body against his as she kissed her way from his chest to…

Arousal settled low and deep and burned hot in his belly. He held back a groan of pure pleasure the image evoked.

He laced his fingers with hers, then brought them to his mouth, lightly skimming his lips over the back of her hand. He should lie, he thought. He should tell her she was imagining his labored breathing, that the hard ridge of his desire pressing insistently against the button fly of his jeans was nothing more than an erotic figment of her imagination.

He should save his hide while he still had the chance to escape unscathed.

*Your hide? Or your heart?*

"What signs are those?" he asked, effectively ignoring his conscience and downing his good intentions in one fell swoop. Nothing like throwing accelerant on already glowing embers.

The blue and green of her eyes blended together into a brilliant shade of turquoise. The gold rims surrounding her irises flared to life, adding a whole lot of heat to her smoldering expression.

A playful smile filled with wicked intent curved her luscious mouth and she pulled her hand free of his grasp. The tips of her fingers feathered against his chest, then traveled with agonizing slowness down his torso, stopping when she reached the top button of his jeans.

He made the monumental error of looking down, of following the path of her fingers. Teasingly, she flicked her fingernail against the metal button. Air whooshed out of his lungs in a rush. For the life of him, he couldn't draw his next breath.

Her sexy brand of torture continued as she drew a lazy circle around the top button, then daringly dipped the tip of her middle finger behind the denim placket. She moistened her bottom lip with the edge of her tongue, then tapped her nail against the second metal button.

Breathing took a back seat to the deafening pounding of his own heartbeat. He fought to remain standing because he was damned close to dropping to his knees, begging her to make love to him, and to hell with the consequences.

So much for all his good intentions.

"Oh," he managed, surprised he still had the capacity for speech. "That sign."

That wicked smile of hers widened as she slid her finger down to the third metal button, adding the barest hint of pressure. "I'm so glad we understand each other."

His body flexed so hard in response, his thinning control nearly unraveled this time. "Are you sure about this?"

*Please, God, don't let her change her mind now.*

She nodded. "I've never been more sure of anything."

"That's not saying much," he said with a soft chuckle.

One of her cinnamon eyebrows arched slightly. "I'm serious."

"So am I." He sobered. "What if—?"

The fingers peeking out from her cast pressed against his lips, halting his argument.

"Shh," she hushed him. "No more 'what if' or 'what about.' I've done nothing but play the game and I'm sick to death of it. What if I never remember anything substantial about my life? What if I don't like the person I discover is the real me? What about tomorrow? What about yesterday?"

She drew in a deep breath and let it out slowly. "All I have are bits and pieces of a past I cannot even

honestly claim is mine. My future is as much an unknown as the past. But I can have the present. I need
that, Cale. I need this moment. I need it with you."

In the face of her convincing argument, words
failed him. She was absolutely right. Either they
could dwell on unknowns or enjoy what time they
had left together. No matter which way he looked at
the situation, he knew without a doubt that once
Maggie regained her memory, she'd no longer need
him and would have to return to her life. Did he really want to squander what precious moments they
had left agonizing over matters he couldn't possibly
control?

Gently, he reached for her, cupping her face between his palms before tenderly tasting her lips.
"You're right," he admitted, kissing her again. "We
do have the present, so let's not waste another minute
of it."

Maggie wreathed her arms around Cale's waist,
certain she'd never heard sweeter words. "Now
you're talkin'," she murmured against his mouth,
then parted her lips and welcomed him inside.

Acute awareness powered her senses. The colors
brighter, the scents more bold, as if she'd been struck
by a surge of electrical intensity increasing the sexual
energy around them. The warm and sweet taste of his
mouth became hotter and more demanding as his
tongue mated with hers. The gentle glide of his hands
into her hair and down her back turned into an insis-
tent quest to bring their bodies closer together.

The warmth of the sun beat down on them through
the latticed roof of the patio, adding even more heat

to her already simmering body. She clung to him. Tasting. Touching. Wanting more. Needing him.

Abruptly, he ended the kiss and lifted his head, his half-lidded gaze filled with sensual intent. "Not here," he said, his voice ragged.

The protest hovering on her lips stilled as the sound of voices drifted over the back fence. "Where?" she asked, not embarrassed in the least by the note of desperation in her voice.

He snagged her hand and pulled her into the house, heading straight for the downstairs guest room. The cats lay twisted together on the full-sized bed beneath the rays of sunlight streaming through the windows, oblivious to the intrusion.

With her hand still clasped in his, he approached the bed and nudged the mattress with his knee. "Scoot," he ordered gently, ushering the lounging felines from the bed. The second the two black-and-white balls of fluff bolted from the room, Cale kicked the door shut with his foot and dragged her back into his arms. "No more interruptions," he said as his mouth sought hers.

The need to touch him, to explore that tempting landscape she'd fantasized about overcame her. With a gentle tug, she pulled his shirt from the waistband of his jeans, then slipped her good hand beneath the material.

Encouraged by his low moan of pleasure, she smoothed her palm over his belly, loving the way the taut muscle danced in response to her touch. She continued upward to curl her fingers in the light furring of hair on his chest, cataloging and savoring the variety of textures of his body.

He broke their kiss long enough to yank his shirt over his head and toss it aside to land in a heap somewhere behind her. A hushed gasp of delight escaped her at the sight of all that warm male flesh exposed just for her pleasure. He reached for her, but she urged him back against the wall, then plastered her body against his.

She nipped and soothed, tasted and laved his tightened nipples, then slowly worked her way down to his washboard-lean belly. She breathed in the tantalizing scent of musk and man, then blew a steady stream of breath where her tongue had been, watching in amazement when gooseflesh puckered beneath the moistened skin.

His large warm hands settled on her shoulders. As she wound a path with her tongue down his remarkable torso, she felt the press of his fingers in her flesh. Whether to hold her back or urge her downward, she couldn't be sure, but when her tongue whorled the rim of his navel, she heard his sharp intake of breath followed by the thump of his head against the wall.

Button by button, she unfastened the fly of his jeans, then boldly slipped her hand beneath the band of his black boxer-briefs. With him hot and heavy in her hand, she struggled to shed the remainder of his clothes, but the cast impeded her progress. She let out a frustrated whimper of need. If she didn't taste him soon, if she didn't feel the length of him against her tongue now, she'd surely go insane.

Cale nearly came out of his skin at the sound of

Maggie's soft peal as she attempted to free him from the strict confines of his briefs. The weight of her cast pressed insistently against his side, so he let go of her shoulders long enough to shove the remaining garments past his hips. Warm breath brushed against his erection as she yanked the jeans down his legs and shoved them aside.

"You are so beautiful." The awe in her voice as she took him in her hand sent him teetering close to the brink. When she teased the tip of his erection with her thumbnail, seductively rubbing it across and back, his knees threatened to buckle.

The slow burn of desire made him a willing casualty to her complete and utter control over him. She settled to her knees in front of him, and his breath stilled. The first feathery brush of her moist tongue against his penis nearly stopped his heart. When she gently drew him into her mouth, it was such an incredible combination of excruciating pain and wild pleasure, he knew he'd died, zipped past purgatory and shot straight into heaven.

A part of him wanted to stop the exquisite torture, to guide her body up his and shed the clothes still hiding her lush curves from his view. The part of him dangerously close to losing control wouldn't dream of putting an end to her selfless lovemaking.

Nothing else mattered now except the moist warmth of her mouth teasing him, loving him, pushing him that much closer to fulfillment. His body tensed and shook. Blood roared in his ears and rushed through his veins. Breathing took a back seat to the primal need for the ultimate satisfaction.

Still, he tried to rein in the need clawing at his belly, to pull back from her before he came. Heaven help him, she pushed his hands away and took him deeper inside.

He closed his eyes, and the world exploded.

His first cognizant thought was the sound of his own ragged breathing, followed by the dangerously erratic beat of his heart. Slowly, he opened his eyes as Maggie kissed and laved first his belly, then his chest and finally wound her arms around his neck and brought his mouth down to hers for a deep, tongue-tangling kiss.

He slipped his hands over her denim-clad rump and lifted her, giving her no choice but to wrap her legs around his waist and hold on tight. Even through the material separating them, her nipples beaded and rubbed enticingly against his chest. But he wanted so much more. He wanted her naked and writhing beneath him, his body buried within hers.

With her still in his arms, he carried her to the bed where he planned to love her for the rest of the day.

Maggie's mind whirled and her body swam in a pool of desire as Cale set her to her feet, then gently lifted her arms and carefully removed her top. The ugly white cotton bra joined the shirt on the floor near their feet. She toed off her sneakers while he made short work of her jeans, sweeping them down her legs along with the plain white panties. He shoved them aside, then urged her to lift her foot so he could remove the socks covering her feet.

She wanted him desperately.

She needed him inside her.

The tempo of her pulse accelerated when his work-roughened hands slid over her calves and up the back of her thighs to her bottom. She looked down at him still crouched in front of her while his hands gently massaged her backside, the tips of his long fingers inching slowly toward her dewy center.

His breath drifted warm and sweet across moist curls, and she braced herself for the onslaught of passion his intimate kiss would bring. Yet, he hesitated, although his touch filled her with a delicious hunger.

He placed a tender kiss on her abdomen and urged her thighs to part. Her entire body trembled in anticipation and she gripped the round, low post of the bed for support, else she'd end up in a puddle at his feet.

She was powerless to prevent the whimper from escaping; sheer pleasure rolled through her body in gentle waves as his fingers found the core of her. Her whimper coalesced into a deep moan when he slid his fingers inside her, then slowly retreated to smooth the heated moisture with deliberate measured strokes over her feminine folds. Her body couldn't be any more primed, but that didn't stop him from continuing the sensual, intimate exploration designed to triple the need already stringing her body tight.

His mouth brushed over her curls and she cried out in frustration when he failed to kiss her where she needed to feel the heat of his mouth the most. His low chuckle rumbled deep in his chest. "Don't be so impatient, sweet. We have all day and all night."

Her body flexed around his fingers at the rich, seductive sound of his velvety-smooth voice. "I want you inside me," she whispered. "I need you."

Carefully, he stood and gathered her in his arms. "I...I need you, too."

Her heart gave a sharp tug at the unabashed affection shining in his gorgeous blue eyes. In that very instant she knew they were no longer thinking about physical needs and wants, and although he hadn't said the words, she understood the force guiding them labored on another level entirely. A deeper, emotional one where walking away with her heart intact would take more courage than facing an unknown past and an uncertain future.

But she was here, now, in the present. A present that included Cale because no matter how she tried, she could no longer imagine life without him by her side.

"Make love to me, Cale." Her voice cracked with powerful feelings that she suddenly had no desire to fight. She welcomed the warmth filling her heart and accepted the tenderness banked in his eyes for the simple reason that this very moment in time, with his arms wrapped around her, was all that really mattered.

He answered her demand by lifting her in his arms and following her down onto the mattress. Lovingly, he smoothed the hair from her face, then dipped his head to capture her mouth in a kiss so hot and wet her toes curled.

Delicious sensation zapped her nerve endings as his hands explored every contour of her body. The red-hot haze ignited into a fierce inferno, the flames licking her body when he palmed her breast then flicked his tongue over her taut nipple. He pulled the rosy tip into his mouth and her hips rocked in response to the need simmering in her belly.

His hand slid along her rib cage, over her abdomen and finally, down between her thighs. She opened for him, trusting him to care for her, to give her what her body craved so desperately. Using his fingers, he strummed her body as if he held the finest instrument in his hands. He guided her to that place where light exploded and sensation traveled through her veins at warp speed. She came hard, her back arching off the bed, her hips seeking an even more intimate contact as her body clenched around his fingers.

He leaned over her as she rode the glorious shock-waves of pleasure. He never allowed her body to cool, but instead pushed her toward the edge again. Tension built with rapid insistence and the muscles in her stomach tightened.

"Look at me," he insisted roughly. "I want to see your eyes this time when you come."

She lifted her gaze to his as a second orgasm tore through her body, making her cry out from sheer bliss.

He emitted a low growl of satisfaction. "An opal."

"Hmm?" she murmured. She hoped he wasn't looking for a more verbal response, since an incoherent groan was about all she had the strength to manage.

He slid over her, settled his body between her thighs and entered her. She lifted her hips to meet his, pulling the long, hot length of him deep inside her body, and moaned as he filled her.

His hips rocked against hers, burying himself inside her. "Your eyes," he said, his voice strained. He rose above her, then took hold of her left leg and settled the quivering limb over his strong bicep. He rocked against her again, driving deeper still, heightening her senses beyond anything she ever imagined.

"When you come, the color of your eyes reminds me of an opal."

Words escaped her as her concentration centered on the build-up of pressure and pleasure. Her body tightened around his thick shaft and she struggled for breath. She felt wild, primal and so hot she feared she'd spontaneously combust as he thrust into her again and again, harder and deeper with each loving stroke of his body.

Tension built. Muscles strained. Bodies melded into one until she lost the sensation of where he ended and she began. Together they approached the precipice of satisfaction, falling together in complete and honest bliss, sated by the beauty of opening not just their bodies, but their hearts, as well.

She had no idea how much time had passed, but the sun was casting long shadows over the bedroom walls. He held her against his side, his fingers making lazy circles on her hip.

"Cale?"

"Hmm," he answered drowsily.

She snuggled closer and draped her leg over his thighs. With her head nestled against his chest, she closed her eyes and breathed in the sweet, musky scent of their lovemaking.

"Wow," she whispered, seconds before she fell into a contented slumber.

# 12

*HER FOOTSTEPS were as silent as snowfall on the ancient stone steps leading to her special place. The old abandoned cottage was her safe haven, away from spiteful laughter and hurtful taunts. A place where she could create a world in which she always belonged.*

*She'd heard their whispers and had felt the sting of sudden silence whenever she'd walked by them. For weeks she'd even lied to herself, telling herself it didn't matter what they thought of her.*

*She understood in the larger scheme that their acceptance shouldn't make a difference. Except, the awful gossip they whispered about her hurt. She wasn't one of them, and they made sure she never forgot for a second her father had bought and paid her way into their elite society.*

*Here, in the quiet, dusty rooms of the long-forgotten cottage on the grounds of the centuries-old converted abbey, she'd found a sense of peace. A place that belonged just to her and anywhere her imagination took her.*

*She set her book bag on the dusty stone floor. The old wood chair groaned in protest as she situated herself at the plain oak table she'd set up in front of the window so she'd have plenty of light to work. The chair creaked again and she made a note to sneak some wood oil from the maintenance room for the chair. A lamp would be nice, she thought, but the cottage had never been converted to electricity.*

*She shivered from the cold and damp, tugged her heavy sweater tighter around her and glanced longingly at the stone fireplace in the wall behind her. She imagined a fire blazing in the hearth, a thick oval rug covering the cold floor. Maybe even a cup of steaming cocoa at her elbow and a lazy cat curled on the wide ledge of the window. Extravagances she couldn't afford herself, in case someone discovered her safe haven.*

*She reached into the canvas book bag for her special binder, a plain denim-blue-covered notebook where she allowed herself to escape creatively at every opportunity. After opening the binder, she dug into her bag again for a pen. Cool, soft silk teased her fingertips. She reached deeper, found the square of fabric and retrieved the red silk handkerchief from the bag. As was her habit, she lifted the frayed material to her nose and breathed in the faint, lingering scent of a time filled with happier memories.*

*She gasped as the hankie slipped from her fingers, fluttering slowly to the floor as if it were a feather floating on a gentle breeze.*

*The monogrammed V caught her attention and she stared at it for a moment as an old ache filled her heart. With a determined sigh she reached for the handkerchief, but the more she stretched, the farther away it slipped. With horror, she watched as it disintegrated before her eyes...*

"OKAY, this is getting just a little too weird, even for me."

Cale glanced down at Maggie. She lay stretched

out on the leather sofa, her head supported by his thigh as it had been for the past hour since they'd finished off the last of the greasy tacos Maggie had wanted for supper.

"What's weird?" he asked, lowering the volume on the action flick playing on TV.

She frowned as she looked up at him, confusion banked in her gaze. "I know it's impossible because Debbie told me these books weren't being released for another week or two, but I swear I've already read this one."

The book in question was the latest Adam Lawrence spy thriller. His aunt always received advance reading copies of the latest novels prior to their scheduled release dates. She read each and every one of them, too, and prided herself on knowing which books her regular customers would enjoy. In Cale's opinion, his aunt's attention to the most minute detail was what had made Better Books & Collectibles one of Santa Monica's premier shops on Montana Avenue.

"Maybe you read about it somewhere," he suggested. Growing up, there'd always been magazines about books around the house. Perhaps Maggie had flipped through one of the many trade magazines that usually cluttered his aunt's coffee table.

"Hmm, maybe." She shrugged, but didn't sound convinced.

She returned her attention to the book, but he didn't bother to kick up the volume on the movie since his ability to concentrate on the overdone plot had disintegrated long ago. In fact, he was finding it increasingly difficult to concentrate on much of anything that didn't include Maggie in one form or another.

He toyed with the strands of her long, fiery-red hair spread over his lap. If he wasn't careful, he could get used to this, he thought as he watched a police car on TV crash, then explode into a ball of flames.

The blue digital clock on the DVD player showed half past eight. In less than ten hours, he would report to Trinity Station for his next twelve-hour shift. A stab of resentment pierced him, taking him by surprise. Every minute that ticked by was one less that he'd have with Maggie. He had it bad. Real bad.

*Face it, pal. You like having her around.*

He liked the sight of her wearing nothing but one of his button-down shirts she'd taken from his closet once they'd finally emerged from the guest room late in the afternoon. The thick cotton socks covering her delicate feet made her look even more adorable. Innocent, he mused, but quickly ditched that thought. There'd been nothing innocent about the way she'd made love to him or the way she'd responded to him.

Would she sleep in his bed tonight? The first demanding pull of arousal settled low in his gut. Or would she prefer to maintain the status quo and retreat to the guest room?

He decided he didn't care where she slept, so long as it was beside him.

*Yeah? For how long?*

His conscience was really starting to bug him. No handy answer existed, but at least he could admit, if only to himself, that he liked being with her. A lot.

Once they'd finally emerged from the guest room, there'd been no awkwardness between them, but instead a bond he had yet to fully define. The kind he suspected could quite easily become something rich and everlasting.

All of which confused the hell out of him. The time they did have together would end once she no longer needed him. Then what was he supposed to do? Let her go?

*Then ask her to stay.*

"Did you hear that?" she asked suddenly.

He wrapped a wavy lock of hair around his hand. "Hear what, sweetheart?" he asked cautiously, worried he'd spoken aloud.

She laid the novel open on her tummy and looked up at him, frowning. "That repetitive, clicking sound. It's similar to what I heard the other night."

On the television screen, shots rang out in the classic good-versus-bad-guy battle. "Maybe it was the movie," he suggested, breathing a quick sigh of relief that he hadn't spoken.

She turned her head to watch the set, her frown deepening. "No," she said after a moment. "I don't think so." She shrugged, picked up the book and went back to reading.

He went back to admiring the length of her legs and the shape of her calves.

Not two minutes later, she snapped the book closed and swung her feet to the floor. Frustration lined her gaze. "Dammit. What is that noise?"

In his line of work, when a patient reported hearing voices or noises that weren't there, he normally proceeded with a great deal of caution. With Maggie, he'd begun to accept her episodes as typical and not the least bit alarming. "You're still hearing it?"

She put the book on the table before turning to look at him again. "It won't go away and it's driving me crazy. It's so familiar, but I just can't place the sound."

With a push of the button on the remote, he turned off the television. "What about now?" he asked, hoping the sound from the movie he hadn't really been watching was the culprit and not another wacky incident from her unexplainable past.

She let out a gusty sigh and closed her eyes. After a moment she opened them. "Yes." Annoyance tinged her voice. "But I can't figure it out and I can't shake this feeling that I'm supposed to know what it is."

Every memory, every vision that emerged from her mind carried the threat of her leaving that much sooner. As much as the very idea of losing Maggie filled him with dread, he couldn't ignore the fact he'd promised to help her, even if doing so brought them that much closer to eventually saying goodbye.

"I have an idea," he told her, wishing like hell he didn't feel as if he were signing his own death warrant. "Provided you're willing to give it a shot."

"At this point, I'll try just about anything."

He didn't doubt she would. "Have you ever heard of word association?"

She nodded in response. "Why?" she asked. "Do you think it'd help me figure out what the sound is that I keep hearing?"

He shrugged. "Maybe. But only if you're sure you

feel up to it." The last thing he wanted to do was tax her by adding pressure to what she already put on herself, but he couldn't stand to see her so miserable and confused.

"Absolutely." She scooted to the opposite end of the sofa and rested her back against the thickly padded leather arm. With her legs crossed, she snagged one of the throw pillows and hugged it to her chest. "I'm ready. Especially if it means getting rid of that stupid noise rattling around in my head."

"Are you relaxed?" he asked. He was completely turned on, but kept that thought to himself. Now was not the time for another sensual exploration, no matter how tempting.

His body had other ideas, so he moved into a more comfortable position.

She closed her eyes and pulled in a few deep breaths. Finally, her lashes fluttered open and she smiled. "Okay, I'm ready."

He decided to start with the basics to see where it led them. "Boy."

Her lips twitched. "Man."

"Woman."

A grin filled with enough wicked sensuality to start his pulse pounding spread across her adorable face. "Sex."

"Maggie."

Her sweet laughter filled the room as she pointedly ignored the warning note in his voice. "You were supposed to say *yes*."

The thought had crossed his mind—and made his body flex in response.

"Okay, okay." She tossed the pillow aside, straightened her shoulders and pushed up her shirt-sleeves. "Let's try again."

"Woman." And what a woman, he thought, unable to keep his eyes off all that bare skin peeking out under the hem of his shirt.

"Mother," she countered.

"Father."

A soft gasp escaped her lips and her eyes widened. Apprehension filled him. "What is it?" he asked.

She nibbled her bottom lip. "The first word that popped into my head was *thief*." A wealth of caution tinged her voice. "Let's keep going."

The slight frown creasing her brow had him hesitating, but she waved her hands at him in a little shooing motion for him to continue. "Thief," he said, against his better judgment.

"Art."

"Museum."

Her frown deepened. "Blueprints."

How she managed to pull *blueprints* from *museum* he couldn't say, but damned if he wasn't intrigued by her response. "Building plans."

"Security system."

"Security system?"

"Uh-huh," she nodded slowly. "As in, using the building plans to determine the layout of the museum's security system."

He couldn't deny she'd told him some strange tales recently, but he felt more than a stab of nervousness about where this game was heading. Especially considering the conclusion he'd drawn last night. "We should stop."

"Not a chance," she said emphatically. "I want to know where this is going."

He wasn't exactly sure he agreed. What was it he'd said about Maggie and endless possibilities? He relented in the face of her sheer determination. "It's your call." he finally said, but decided to shift the focus to a less-incriminating subject.

"Animal."

She gave him a stern look and folded her arms. "What does animal have to do with security systems?"

"Not a damned thing," he told her. "Humor me, okay?"

She cleared her throat, but eyed him suspiciously. "Fine. Dog."

"Cat."

Her sharp gasp made him decidedly nervous. "What?"

"Burglar," she answered carefully. A blanket of sadness entered her eyes, turning them a pale shade of blue. "Oh, Cale. I think my father is a cat burglar."

He tried to laugh it off, but the sound was more strangled than humorous. "Stop kidding around," he told her, but he had a feeling she was dead serious.

"I'm not. Think about it for a minute." She reached for the throw pillow and hugged it to her chest again. "The dreams, the memory I had yesterday. You can't tell me it doesn't add up. My father is, or maybe was, a thief."

She hesitated, looking away. "And I took the fall for him."

"No." He shot off the sofa and started pacing the room hoping to dispel the edginess he felt. "You can't believe that." No matter how much he wished he could discount her theory, even he had to admit, on the surface, it didn't look good.

"Why not?" she argued. "The glass wall, me being led away by someone. My father mouthing an apology. I remember feeling afraid for him for being there."

"Being where, Maggie?" He stopped pacing and faced her. "Where were you?" he demanded.

He was sure he already knew the answer. Dammit, he wanted her to deny the nagging suspicion that hadn't completely left his mind since he'd drawn his own conclusions about the information she'd imparted before he'd gone to work last night.

"Prison."

Memories and emotion flooded Maggie, racing through her mind with such lightning speed she was powerless to catalog them all. Except one that stood head and shoulders above the rest...her worst fears had just been realized.

Cale stood in the middle of the living room, his hands braced on his hips, staring at her as if she'd lost her mind. Maybe she had this time. How could she believe otherwise when the memories swamping her were too vivid to be anything but reality?

He leveled her with his gaze and she watched in amazement as he wrestled with the truth.

"No," he said after a moment. "I'm not buying it. It's just not possible. Not the Maggie I know."

"I wish I could agree with you, but I can't."

He circled the table and dropped onto the leather sofa next to her. "I'll admit I drew a similar conclusion, but sweetheart, it can't be true. There isn't a corrupt bone in that beautiful body of yours."

She appreciated his staunch support of her moral fiber, but the truth of the matter wasn't quite so simple. "I'm definitely a chip off the old cell block, and I learned my trade from the best in the business...renowned jewel thief James LaRue."

His mouth fell open as her words registered.

She knew the feeling.

"Wait a minute," he said. "Back up. Learned *your* trade?"

As much as it pained her to do so, she nodded. God help her, she'd wanted to learn the truth, and now she had, she wished her memory had remained forever hidden. "We used to work together. The family business, he used to call it."

"And what was your mother? The ring leader?"

She didn't appreciate his sarcasm, but she could hardly blame him. After all, she'd just admitted to a life of crime.

"I don't think she was around," she said, overcome by a wealth of sadness she had yet to understand. Had her parents divorced? Or had her mother passed away? The answer eluded her, but that didn't quell the sense of loss clinging to the fringes of her mind.

"We've been over this ground before, Maggie. You are *not* a criminal."

She opened her mouth to disagree, but he shot her a dark look filled with frustration, effectively stilling the argument hovering on her lips.

"How did you supposedly end up in prison?" he demanded.

She traced her finger over the binding of the pillow she held to her chest. "The Arden Collection."

He leaned forward, bracing his elbows on his knees. "Never heard of it," he said, the skepticism in his tone obvious.

"It's a collection of rare Egyptian jewels the Arden family loaned to...oh, I can't remember where, but the family allowed the collection to be put on public display. Henri Arden was an archeologist back in the thirties, credited with unearthing the tomb of an Egyptian princess. Only it wasn't Arden who actually discovered the tomb, but his partner Phillipe Wendell, whom I might add died rather mysteriously."

The words flowed from her with such ease, she had no choice but to trust their authenticity. "Legend has it that Arden murdered Wendell and took credit for the find. James LaRue was hired by..." She tapped her fingers on the pillow, struggling to call up a name. "I can't remember that, either, but I'm pretty sure he's a grandson or grandnephew of Wendell. Anyway, he hired us to recover the collection and return it to the Wendell family."

She attempted to gauge his reaction. He remained remarkably stoic; she wanted to squirm. Silence stretched between them. God, she wished he'd say something.

He smiled. The man had the audacity to smile at

her. Just a little tug of his lips, but a smile nonetheless. "Do you have any idea how ridiculous you sound?"

She didn't appreciate the condescending tone of his voice one iota. "Of course I do." Sure, she knew her story sounded absolutely insane. The fact that she couldn't deny it made her feel perfectly crazy, too. And at least a half dozen cards shy of a full deck. "But it's all in here." She tapped her index finger against her temple, half expecting to hear an echo.

No matter how much she wished otherwise, suddenly it all made perfect sense, especially when she factored in the dream she'd had that afternoon when she'd fallen asleep in Cale's arms. The sense of not belonging hadn't been because the blood running through her veins wasn't blue, or even that she'd been one generation away from white trash in the eyes of the girls at the boarding school. They'd scorned her because she was the daughter of James LaRue.

Unlike the other memories of her past, the realization she'd gone to boarding school hardly came as a surprise. More like acceptance, she thought, wondering at the difference.

Cale's hand settled over her knee, drawing her attention to the warmth against her skin. His expression patient, he asked, "You said you took the fall for your dad. How?"

She thought for a minute, waiting for the answer to come to her. "He made a mistake," she said eventually, not one-hundred-percent certain she was right. "I created a diversion so he could get out."

"You want me to believe you were busted, sent to

prison and now you're walking around free? At least there'd be a record of your fingerprints."

"Yes. Why won't you believe me?" The fingerprint argument stumped her, too.

His frown turned ferocious. "Because dammit, I..." The anger in his expression dissipated as quickly as it arose, replaced by tenderness and something else she could only name as fear. "Because I care about you."

Caring wasn't the same as loving, but the tenderness and fear in his eyes said what he could not voice.

His fingers drew a lazy circle over her knee. "How long ago did this happen?"

When he touched her like that, her ability for coherent thought tended to evaporate. "I'm not sure. Why?"

"You can't be any older than twenty-six, maybe twenty-nine tops. You couldn't have done more than a couple of years time. I'd bet an attempted robbery of a priceless collection is a serious crime, with a steep sentence."

She shrugged and looked away. "Maybe I was paroled."

"I doubt it." He took the pillow from her and clasped her hand tightly in his. "Sweetheart, I see human nature every day, the good and the bad. Not all the lives I save are upstanding citizens. Trust me on this. You don't have the killer instinct."

Lord, she wanted to believe him, but she was afraid to put stock in the twinge of hope the possibility gave her. The details were simply too specific for her to believe otherwise.

She lifted her gaze to his, awed by the unwavering

conviction shining in his eyes. Her heart stuttered behind her ribs as realization slammed into her and shook her—hard. When was the last time someone close to her had believed in her the way Cale apparently did now?

As with everything else in her life lately, the answer remained out of reach, but she didn't blame her faulty memory. This time she knew for certain the answer lay deep in her heart.

She twisted her hand in his to lace their fingers together. "Then why am I having these memories if they aren't real?" she asked him. "There has to be some truth to them."

With a gentle tug on their joined hands, he urged her closer. He pulled her into his arms, and she clung to him and held on tight, accepting his support and his unconditional belief in her. And yes, even the emotion he could not, or would not, name.

A lump lodged in her throat.

He pulled back and urged her chin up with the tip of his index finger, giving her no choice but to look into his eyes and see the determination there for herself. "I wish I had an answer for you," he said gently. "But I will get one. Somehow, I'm going to find a way to prove you're wrong."

Her heart filled with a warmth that ran right past caring and sprinted straight into territory so virgin it nearly took her breath away. She recognized the feeling and welcomed it into her heart. Into that place Cale had taken up residence when she hadn't been looking because she'd been too busy chasing dreams of a past he refused to believe belonged to her.

She only wished she had his faith.

# 13

By THE END of the week, Cale was no closer to fulfilling his promise to Maggie than when he'd made it. Not only had he not been able to disprove her theories, he hadn't come close to proving them, either. So far as he could tell, her theory about the Arden Collection was the legend behind Howard Carter's 1922 discovery of King Tut's Tomb.

Maybe she was simply confused, he thought, drumming his fingers on the computer desk. A twisted combination of history and some other factor they'd yet to determine.

Trinity Station had remained relatively quiet for most of Friday morning, so he took advantage of the opportunity for another trip down the information highway.

Thanks to the electronic age, he'd found a wealth of facts at his fingertips, but every search he'd conducted thus far had been fruitless. He'd searched the online archives of old newspaper articles from the country's biggest publications and come up with nothing. No Arden Collection seemed to exist, nor could he find details on a seventy-five-year-old archeological expedition that resulted in the supposedly famed collection, other than what he'd already found on Carter's dramatic discovery. Surely if there was some truth behind Maggie's story, even a small amount of information would exist on the subject.

He ignored the sound of male laughter coming from the kitchen, logged on and started his search. Thirty minutes later, he knew as much about James LaRue as when he'd started. Maggie claimed her father was a renowned jewel thief. If he was so damn well-known, why the hell couldn't he find an ounce of data on the guy?

He leaned back in the chair and laced his hands together behind his head.

*My name is Maggie LaRue.*

"Hey, Cale?" Brady called from the kitchen. "You gonna eat or what?"

"Be there in a minute," he answered, then leaned forward and started another search. Even though Maggie had told him she'd already tried to confirm her identity online, he decided to cover the same ground.

Slowly he straightened. The search wouldn't lead him to solid answers because...

*Because I got it off a headstone.*

Her words had him sitting back and staring at the computer screen again. If she'd gotten the name off a headstone as she'd claimed, then what she'd said about her father made no sense. Even if she'd changed her name to escape a shady past, then how was it possible her "new" persona still shared the same last name as her father?

A slow grin spread across his mouth. Two and two had just equaled five.

If Maggie LaRue was the name of a dead woman, then James LaRue, couldn't be her father. So, if she wasn't Maggie LaRue, exactly who was the woman who'd stolen his heart?

Ben set a plate with a corned beef sandwich on rye and a heaping serving of potato salad on the desk next to the keyboard. "If the mountain doesn't come to what's-his-name."

Cale scratched the back of his head and looked up at his brother. "Excuse me?"

Ben inclined his head toward the plate of food. "Your order," he said, handing him an icy-cold can of soda. "Fitz was about to claim it."

"Thanks." Cale popped open the top of the can and took a long drink.

Using his foot for balance, Ben sat on the edge of the desk and leaned forward, bracing his forearm on his thigh. "What's got you so distracted?"

"Nothing is making sense," Cale said, openly frustrated. "I haven't been able to find a single shred of evidence on any of the stuff Maggie's told me about herself."

Ben frowned. "You don't trust her?"

"No, that's not it." The facts were such a tangled mess, he wasn't sure where to begin.

"Then what is it?" Ben pushed.

Cale set the soda on the desk and glanced around the day room before giving Ben his full attention. "I don't think anything she's told me about herself is true," he said, keeping his voice low.

"She's been lying to you?"

Cale shook his head. "No. She's not *lying*," he clarified. "I think she really believes what she's been telling me, but I'm starting to doubt the memories are real."

More laughter erupted from the kitchen, but Cale ignored it and quietly told Ben what he'd learned, or rather what he hadn't been able to confirm. He finished by explaining how even the agency Maggie claimed to work for—S.E.C.S.—as far as he could tell, was also nonexistent.

Ben stared down at the worn carpet and remained thoughtful.

"Any brilliant ideas?" Cale asked, hopeful. "I'm not sure what else to do other than wait for her memory to return."

Ben lifted his head and looked at him, his eyes filled with his usual concern. "Waiting is all you can do since pushing her to remember is out of the question."

Cale let out a long frustrated breath. Obviously, he and Ben thought a lot alike.

"You know," Ben said as he slid off the edge of the desk and stood, "it's not your job to save her."

Well, on some subjects anyway.

Cale didn't agree, not when she had no one else to turn to. She needed him. "I have to do something."

Instead of fighting with Cale or spewing a lengthy lecture he wouldn't listen to anyway, Ben surprised him by shrugging his shoulders and walking away.

Alone again, Cale bent over the keyboard and started typing a new string of connected phrases into the appropriate box of the search engine.

His hands stilled over the keyboard.

He swallowed hard, then typed again, paying close attention to the repetitive clicking sound as he typed.

"Well, I'll be damned," he muttered.

He abandoned the search engine and called up the notepad, then began typing random sentences. His speed left a little to be desired compared to the way Maggie's fingers flew over the keyboard each evening when she wrote down her dreams and visions, hoping for clarity. But the rhythmic clicking she'd described the night he'd suggested they try word association to help stir her memory was of her fingers on the keys of a computer.

*I could swear I've read this one already.*

He straightened and shook his head, not sure whether to trust his instincts. *No way,* he thought. The idea settling in his mind was simply too far out there to be real. Obviously his imagination was becoming as creative as Maggie's.

Still, he couldn't shake the thought from his mind, or the hope from his heart. He reached for his cell phone and punched in the speed dial code for his aunt's bookstore.

Within seconds, Maggie's voice was on the other end. Damn. In his excitement at his possible discovery, he'd forgotten she was working today. "Hey there," he said, aiming for a neutral tone. He wasn't about to say anything to her until he confirmed his suspicions.

Her sweet laughter washed over him. "Hey there, yourself," she said. "I was just thinking about you."

The husky undertone of her voice set off a series of

sparks guaranteed to coax his libido into a blazing inferno. "I think I'm afraid to ask why."

She made a low purring sound that heated his
blood.

"Are we about to have phone sex?" he teased. "Because I should warn you, I'm not alone."

She laughed again, making him smile. "The
thought is tempting, but no. I was going to call and
tell you not to pick me up tonight. Debbie's giving me
the afternoon off, and Tilly and I are going shopping.
She wants a new dress for a hot date tomorrow
night."

Apparently his friend had agreed to go out with
Scorch. For Scorch's sake, he hoped the guy didn't
hurt Tilly.

"And what do you want?" He knew her wants as
well as his own, which did nothing to cool his rising
temperature.

"Hmm," she murmured in a low sexy voice. "If I
told you now, we could both get into trouble."

He chuckled softly. Lord, the woman excited him
beyond belief. "I don't doubt that," he said, imagining all sorts of wicked scenarios they could explore
together. "Actually, I called to talk to Debbie. Is she
there?"

"She's in the back. Just a minute."

For every second that ticked by while he waited for
his aunt to pick up the line, his anticipation climbed a
notch. What if he was right? What was he supposed
to do then?

"Cale!" Debbie came on the line, saving him from

searching for the answers to his own questions. "What a lovely surprise."

"I need you to look something up for me," he quickly told his aunt. "Can you spare a minute?"

"Sure," she said. He didn't miss the curiosity in her voice. "Just tell me what you need."

"Do you have any Adam Lawrence novels on hand?"

"As a matter of fact, I'm unpacking his newest release as we speak. Why?"

"I need to know who owns the copyright."

"Hold on a minute."

He closed his eyes and waited.

Debbie came back on the line. "ADH, Inc."

He opened his eyes and shoved his hand through his hair. "Damn. Do you know where to get information on corporation filings? I've got a hunch about something and I want to check it out."

Debbie hesitated for a moment. "The Secretary of State's office," she said eventually. "Cale? Does this have something to do with Maggie?"

"It might," he confessed. "Don't say anything to her, though. I'd rather wait until I have proof."

Once Debbie agreed, Cale disconnected the call, anxious to begin his next search. He started with the California office of the Secretary of State, astounded by the information available via the Internet. Working his way across the map, he narrowed his search by selecting only those states with major metropolitan areas. If he turned up nothing, then he'd search his way back through every state in the union if necessary.

On his third option, he hit pay dirt. Listed as a corporation within the state of New York was ADH, Inc. His heart began a slow, heavy beat in his chest. All he had to do was click on the link for agent of service of process and he just might discover the information necessary to set Maggie free from a confused past that he'd bet didn't even exist in the first place.

He scrolled over to the link and clicked the button on the mouse. The Web page listing the agent for service of process appeared on the monitor. He let out the breath he hadn't even realized he'd been holding as he read the name on the screen.

ADH, Inc., otherwise known as best-selling spy thriller novelist, Adam Lawrence, was the pen name for Amanda Darnell Hayes of Manhattan.

"So, ARE YOU sleeping with Cale?"

Maggie nearly tripped as she returned the pale yellow cotton jumper to the sale rack. With her hand wrapped firmly around the metal bar to steady herself, she slowly turned to face Tilly. "I'm not sure how to answer that question."

Tilly laughed knowingly. "I think you just did."

Heat crept up Maggie's neck and burned her cheeks.

"Don't be embarrassed," Tilly chided gently. "I grew up with Cale, remember? Besides, you make him happy."

Then why couldn't he tell her that himself? All week long, they'd spent every possible moment together, and not once had he told her what she knew was in his heart. He constantly showed her in a variety of ways, from the mint chocolate chip ice cream he'd brought home from work last night to helping her wash her hair because the cast kept her from doing a good job of it herself. He'd even taken her shopping for more clothes so she could have something other than blue jeans to wear to work. But he hadn't said he loved her, and she was beginning to believe him incapable of saying the words her heart longed to hear.

"Where is Tom taking you?" Maggie asked, deliberately changing the subject.

Behind her, Tilly searched another rack of sale items. They'd been to three stores already and nothing had caught her eye. "Dinner and the theater," she said. "What do you think?"

Relieved Tilly had taken the hint, Maggie turned and examined the simple but elegant dress with a sweetheart neckline and cap sleeves that Tilly held up in front of her. The flirty hem reached about three inches above Tilly's knee.

"I think red is definitely your color." With Tilly's dark sable hair and rich chocolate eyes, the color was absolutely stunning. "I always have to go with black," Maggie said with a touch of envy.

Tilly walked around the circular rack to the mirror-covered column. "Not too sexy?" She slipped the hanger over her head and held the dress against her body. "I don't want to give the wrong impression."

"Here's a black one that's nice. But I thought this was a *hot* date."

Tilly examined the dress Maggie held, then wrinkled her nose. "I think I like the red one."

"Then red it is," Maggie agreed and returned the black dress to the rack.

Tilly's hand clutched her shoulder suddenly, making her jump. "Maggie? Do you realize what you just said a minute ago."

*"Then red it is,"* Maggie repeated with a shrug.

Tilly leaned closer. "No," she said in a hushed tone. "You said that you always have to go with black."

"It's not a great mystery," Maggie said with a laugh. "How many redheads do you see actually wearing red?"

"Okay," Tilly agreed sheepishly. "But I deserve credit for paying attention."

Once Tilly had tried on the dress and realized it was perfect, she paid for it then insisted on making a quick stop at the lingerie shop before they left the mall, claiming she needed red lingerie to wear under her new dress.

"The only impression you're going to make is a lasting one," Maggie said as they entered the shop. Lingerie had been the one thing she hadn't looked for on her trip to the mall with Cale. Regardless of how silly it was, she just hadn't been comfortable shopping for lacy, feminine undergarments with a man around, especially one who was temporarily footing the bill.

Lace demi bras, thongs and boy-short panties in nearly every color imaginable covered neat round tables spread throughout the store. Headless, armless, legless mannequins were perched atop tables sporting water, push-up and full-figure bras.

Maggie might not care much for the plain white cotton undergarments she'd been wearing, but the pearl thong she spied was a bit much. Still, thanks to her first paycheck from the bookstore, she had a few extra dollars and couldn't wait to indulge herself with something sleek and sexy...and one-hundred percent guaranteed to drive Cale to his knees.

Maggie nudged Tilly. "Over there."

Tilly dropped the electric-blue satin thong back on the display table. "Heart-attack city, here he comes." She wiggled her eyebrows, then laughed as she led the way through the tables and racks to a corner display splashed in vibrant shades of red.

Maggie fingered a silk camisole artfully displayed, wondering if it came in black, or perhaps a soft shade of cream. As she smoothed her hand over a red chemise with a lace inset designed to reveal cleavage and a whole lot more, she spied a red satin garter belt. "What do you say?" she asked Tilly, indicating her find. "Is it you?"

Tilly giggled despite the hesitation in her eyes. "Not really. But since you're predicting a lasting impression..."

Tilly disappeared into the dressing room after making a few selections from the display, the garter belt included, leaving Maggie to meander through the shop alone. Conscious of her budget, she approached a mirrored wall in the back of the store in search of sale items. Instead she found a rainbow of silk scarves arranged with bottles of edible body lotions in a variety of exotic flavors. She couldn't help wondering if Cale would prefer coconut cream or white chocolate raspberry.

A bright pink heart-shaped box beside the lotions displayed neatly placed lace, satin and silk handkerchiefs. She trailed her fingers over the mixed textures of fabric, then slipped a red hankie from the box and brought it to her cheek. She breathed in deeply, but there was no soft, lingering aroma of her mother's vanilla-scented perfume.

Her legs trembled and she fought for breath.

Blindly, she reached for the display counter to steady herself.

Her ears buzzed.

Her vision blurred.

Her heart raced.

*Her mind flooded with memories.*

She'd been twelve when she'd lost her mother to a long battle with breast cancer. The day of the funeral, her heartbroken father had instructed the housekeeper to pack up his wife's things. She remembered the awful ache in her chest when she'd gone into her mother's dressing room afterward only to find there was nothing left. All the memories had been packed up and donated to charity in a matter of hours. Everything except the single, monogrammed red silk handkerchief she'd found caught in the drawer of her mother's bureau. A beautiful, delicate script *V* in the corner above the lace edging. A *V* for Virginia Adams Hayes.

"Maggie?"

Tilly's voice barely penetrated the memories lashing out at her. The lonely years spent at the English boarding school her stepmother had insisted she attend. The arguments with her father when she'd walked away from an Ivy League education to attend a small liberal arts college in upstate New York. The secretarial job she'd hated but suffered through while she sold her first few novels. The ache caused by her father's initial disappointment when he'd discovered she hadn't been toiling away on the Great American Novel or the next landmark work of literary fiction destined for a Nobel, but on spy thrillers with mass-market appeal.

She felt someone take her arm and lead her to the pink velvet settee near the changing rooms.

Tilly pushed her down, then crouched in front of her. "Maggie? What's wrong?"

She blinked several times before she looked at Tilly. "Mandy," she said. Her throat felt as dry as dust.

Tilly frowned. "Excuse me?"

She cleared her throat. "Actually, it's Amanda. The only person that ever calls me Mandy is Ella, my father's housekeeper."

"Oh, my God. You remember," Tilly said in whispered awe.

"Everything," she admitted. "My apartment in New York. The reason I was in that warehouse two weeks ago. All of it."

Tilly gave her arm a gentle squeeze. "Are you okay?" she asked, her eyes still filled with concern.

"I will be. I think I'm in shock right now." She laughed, but the sound was more brittle than humorous.

"No doubt."

"Would you mind taking me home?"

Tilly eyed her suspiciously. "We should probably get you over to the hospital. I know you were kidding about the shock, but it's not an unrealistic response, considering."

"No." At her abrupt response, the sales clerk glanced curiously in their direction. Amanda would've stood, but her legs were still trembling. "I need to see Cale." She lowered her voice. "He has to know."

Tilly didn't look convinced. She pulled a bottle of water from the tote slung over her shoulder and handed it her. "Drink this, then we'll leave."

Amanda took the bottle and drank deeply. "Go pay for your stuff. I'll wait here."

By the time Tilly returned, the trembling had stopped. Even the ringing in her ears had diminished to a dull thrum.

"I have to know," Tilly said, hovering cautiously as they left the lingerie shop. "Who is Maggie LaRue?"

Amanda cringed with embarrassment. The grin she gave Tilly was weak at best. "She's the main character of my next book."

# 14

ADRENALINE pumped through Cale's veins as he and Brady walked through the door of the small house located in one of Santa Monica's oldest residential districts. They were met by the distinct odors of mothballs and lemon furniture wax and, God help them...death.

"She's in there." A woman in her mid-forties with red-rimmed eyes and a crumpled tissue in her hands pointed toward the hallway. "My father's with her."

Cale knew the way and took off down the hallway toward the master bedroom. The call had come in ten minutes after his shift was supposed to have ended. Since he'd recognized the address as one of their most frequent flyers, Sheila Eames, an eighty-seven-year-old lung cancer patient, he and Brady had taken the call rather than sending in the next team of paramedics on duty.

Cale approached the bed, set his kit on the floor, then sat on the edge and faced Sheila. Brady hovered in the background, his tone soothing as he spoke with Sheila's daughter.

"How are you doing today, Sheila?"

Her smile might have been frail, but there was staunch determination in her still-sharp hazel eyes despite the horrible gurgling sound in her chest. "I'm not going with you," she rasped with effort.

Cale took her vitals and quickly determined she would indeed be going to the emergency room today. Not only was her temperature elevated, her pulse weak and thready, but her oxygen saturation level had dropped to less than eighty percent.

He calmly held her arthritic hand between his and smiled at her. "I'm going to start an IV, Sheila, and then we're going to transport you to the hospital."

With monumental effort, Sheila pulled in as deep a breath as her tired body could manage. "Not today."

A gnarled hand fell on Cale's shoulder. He glanced up to see Sheila's husband, Richard, standing beside him. "Leave her be," he said, as he lovingly gazed at his dying wife. "It's her time now."

Determination filled Cale. Her time? Not on his watch. His job was to sustain life, and that's exactly what he planned to do.

"I don't think you understand what you're saying."

"I understand perfectly," the older gentleman said in a matter-of-fact tone. "My wife doesn't wish to leave her home."

Cale carefully settled Sheila's hand back on the soft, faded handmade quilt and stood. He signaled to Brady, who immediately stepped forward to watch over their patient, then steered Richard Eames into the hallway where his wife wouldn't overhear what Cale had to say.

"She needs to be in the hospital, Mr. Eames. Her condition is critical. You'll lose her if we don't transport her right away." Cale knew there were no guarantees the doctors could save her this time, but he refused to voice his opinion. Right now, his sole intent was to do his job and help the patient.

Eames lifted his hand and placed it over his heart. "How can I lose someone who'll always be in here?"

Frustration nipped at Cale. Dammit. "Then why did you place a 911 call?"

"I didn't. My daughter called. She's having a difficult time letting go."

Obviously Eames didn't suffer from the same malady. Cale had been called to Eames's residence enough to know a little about the couple. They'd been married for over sixty years. Had Eames tired of the exhausting heartbreak of coping with a long terminal illness? There had to be a logical reason why he refused to convince his wife to allow them to transport her.

Without a DNR, if Sheila had been unconscious when he and Brady arrived, Cale would've had no choice but to treat her, despite her husband's wishes to the contrary. He had the power to help her, yet his hands were tied.

Cale's temper flared. "Mr. Eames," he said forcefully, "Sheila will die if you don't let us take her to the hospital. Do you understand?"

An almost serene expression encompassed Richard's deeply weathered face. "I know," he said, his voice the epitome of resolute calm.

Legally, there wasn't a damn thing Cale could do except honor the patient's wishes, a realization that did nothing to lessen the foreign helplessness he felt.

"I don't understand," he said angrily. "If you love your wife—"

"You don't know how much I do love her," Eames interrupted in that same calm, sure voice. "But Sheila doesn't need me holding on to her, not in that way. The greatest love I can give to my wife is to let her go so she can finally be at peace."

Cale shoved his hand through his hair and stared at the older man as if he'd lost his mind.

"Don't misunderstand, son. I need my wife. I don't know what I'm going to do without her. She's been by my side for sixty-five years. Except when I was in the army during the war, I woke up beside her for every day of those sixty-five years. We had two children, buried one of them and made it through hard times together. It's simple, really. I love her enough to let her go. And loving her is more important than my needing her."

A lump the size of a football wedged in Cale's throat. If his life depended on it, he couldn't speak. Thankfully, Brady chose that moment to step into the hallway.

"Mr. Eames," Brady said gently. "Would you like us to give your wife something for the pain?"

Richard Eames nodded. "Thank you," he said. He gave Cale's shoulder a squeeze, then walked back into the bedroom to be with his wife.

Cale hung back and let Brady take over. After receiving approval from the E.R. doc, Brady administered morphine and instructed Sheila's husband not to hesitate to call again if his wife's pain became unbearable.

Cale remained silent and thoughtful on the drive back to the station. Richard Eames's reaction had been eons away from his father's sheer determination to hold on to his wife. He remembered his dad keeping a constant vigil by his mom's hospital bed for the three days it took for her to pass away, never leaving her side, never offering comfort to the sons who waited, knowing their mother was going to die soon. It hadn't mattered to his dad that Mom had been in intense, agonizing pain from the burns that had covered most of her body. All that had mattered was that she not leave him.

The sense of relief Cale had felt when his aunt had come to tell them that his mother had gone to a better place where she would not be in any pain, had been overwhelming. He might not have been able to understand why something so horrible had happened to his mother, but even as an eight-year-old boy, he'd understood on some level that she wouldn't hurt anymore.

If he concentrated hard enough, even now after all these years he could still hear the agonizing pain in the sobs that had wracked his father's body that day. Cale had never doubted his father's love for his mother. But suddenly, he couldn't help wondering if his father hadn't been selfish in refusing to let her go so she could finally find peace.

Brady parked the rig in the bay, but neither of them were in any hurry to move.

"I hate calls like that," Cale admitted.

Brady looked at him, compassion etched in his expression. "We did all we could for her."

All that she'd allow them to do for her, Cale thought. For him, it hadn't been enough. "What would you do?"

"You mean if it was Elise?" Brady asked. Elise was Brady's wife. They'd only been married a couple of months. "I don't know. I wouldn't want her to suffer, that's for sure."

"You wouldn't want to hold on to her for as long as possible?"

Brady shrugged, then slung his arm over the steering wheel. "Well, yeah," he admitted. "I guess I would, but I love her, and if that means doing the same thing Richard Eames did tonight, then so be it."

Cale didn't know what to say, so he kept quiet. But he did know what he had to do, and that was to tell Maggie what he'd learned today. The proof was nowhere near conclusive, but he at least had a name. With his connections in law enforcement, obtaining a copy of Amanda Hayes's driver's license hadn't been a problem.

He wasn't worried that telling her what he'd learned today might not help with the return of her memories, but if she did remember, then she'd no longer need him. Now he finally understood what Richard Eames had been trying to tell him—love was more important than need.

And when it came to Maggie, Cale knew with absolute certainty, he wanted her love.

"THANK YOU, Detective Villanueva," Maggie said, turning when she heard the rattle of Cale's keys. Pearl came barreling through the living room at the sound and barked as Cale walked through the door.

The smile Maggie had been wearing faded. From the look on Cale's face, something was wrong. "Yes," she told the detective, "for another few days at least."

Cale dropped his keys next to the lamp on the table near the door. "Can what for another few days?" he asked, absently bending down to greet Pearl.

She hung up the phone and pulled in a steadying breath that did little to calm the nervous twitters in her tummy. "Call me at this number if they have more questions."

He braced his feet apart and crossed his arms over his chest, his expression unreadable, giving her no clue what he was thinking.

"Going somewhere?"

She gripped the edge of the desk behind her and rested her backside against the antique wood. "Back to New York?" She hadn't meant it to sound like a question. Or maybe she had. Lord knew the thought of leaving Cale had been plaguing her as much as her returning memories.

His blue eyes darkened slightly, leaving her with a thin thread of hope.

"Wanna run that one by me again, sweetheart?"

She pushed off the desk and walked across the room to stand in front of him. Extending her right hand, cast and all, she smiled up at him. "How do you do?" she said when he took her hand. "I'm Amanda Hayes. It's a pleasure to finally meet you."

His grip on her fingers tightened. "You know." His

voice had that same awe-filled tone Tilly had used back in the lingerie shop.

She nodded.

"But how?" he asked, wonder, disbelief and a hint of fear chasing across his chiseled features. "When?"

"A few hours ago. Tilly and I were shopping and everything came rushing back."

She pulled her hand from his and walked to the sofa, then waited for him to join her. Once he settled down beside her, she explained about the handkerchief and how it had jarred whatever had been holding her memories prisoner.

"I called Detective Villanueva to give him information about what I recalled prior to the explosion. That's who I was talking to when you walked in."

She'd called her father first, but Lawrence Hayes hadn't been the least bit surprised to hear from her. Her agent's reaction had been similar—perfectly understandable responses, since she made a habit of going away for weeks at a time when she worked. To their credit, though, when she'd explained her situation, they'd been duly shocked and concerned for her well-being.

The worry in Cale's eyes deepened. "Do you remember the explosion?"

She shook her head. "No," she told him. "There are some things I remember, like how I got inside the warehouse and why I was even there in the first place."

"And?"

Tilly's humorous reaction and her virtually non-stop giggles about the fact that Amanda had been wandering around for days thinking she was a character in one of her books, had done little to ease Amanda's embarrassment. Granted, when she was working on a book, she basically ate, slept and breathed her characters, but never to such a bizarre psychological extent. She wasn't exactly looking forward to explaining it all over again, but Cale deserved to know every last scrap of the truth.

She took another deep breath that did zilch to calm the butterflies tormenting her stomach, then turned to face Cale. "I'd better start at the beginning."

In that unique way he had of sensing her emotions, he reached across the space separating them and laid his hand on her arm in a gesture of comfort. She took strength from his warm touch.

"I'm a writer, Cale." She tried to gauge his reaction, but he showed no outward sign of surprise. "The reason I couldn't shake the feeling that I'd read that Adam Lawrence novel wasn't because I'd read it before." She pulled in another deep breath and let it out slowly. "It was because I'd written it. Adam Lawrence is a pen name. I took my father's first name and a variation of my mother's maiden name."

"I know," he said quietly. "You're ADH, Inc."

"You knew? For how long?" She didn't want to believe he'd withheld something so important from her.

He reached into his shirt pocket and withdrew a folded sheet of paper. "Not until today," he said, carefully opening the paper. "I had a hunch and did some digging. I called in a favor and was able to get this for you."

He handed her the paper and she stared at the

black-and-white driver's license photo. "Yup," she said and set the copy on the pine table. "That's me, all right. Twenty-seven years old, born on St. Patrick's Day. No brothers or sisters, and, other than my father and stepmother, the only other relative I had is a grandmother who passed away four years ago."

She rattled off her personal information as if she'd never lost track of it, every detail as real to her as Cale sitting next to her listening intently.

"I lost my mother when I was twelve and my life changed forever," she told him. "My dad remarried a couple of years later and at my stepmother's insistence, I was shipped off to a prep school abroad. I hated it there, but now I can at least value the education. I attended Yale for a semester but much to my father's horror, I transferred to a small liberal arts college in upstate New York from which I graduated. I never went back for my master's, but it's an idea I've been toying with lately."

"What were you doing in L.A.?" he asked.

Heat crept up her neck and burned her cheeks for the second time that day. "Researching my next novel," she admitted sheepishly. "Uh...I think you might know the character. Her name's Maggie LaRue, a reformed jewel thief."

He didn't laugh, but he did smile. A big one that curved his mouth and brightened his heavenly blue eyes, and didn't hold so much as an ounce of ridicule. "Something tells me it's going to be your next bestseller."

Relief swept through her and she laughed nervously. "You don't think I'm crazy?"

He gave her a sidelong glance, clearing stating the subject was debatable. Okay, she deserved that one. What kind of sane person actually became a character in a book? None that she knew.

"That still doesn't explain why you were in the warehouse," he said.

She let out an exasperated breath and rolled her eyes. "Maggie's father, James, is back and he's smuggling jewels, getting them through customs in cans of paint. Maggie works for S.E.C.S., a *fictional* government agency that walks a thin legal line. When Maggie is busted the night she creates a diversion to save James, she's given the opportunity to become a part of the S.E.C.S. team as a security advisor in exchange for her jail sentence. The caveat is that she must bring down her own father.

"I needed to find out how the paint was warehoused, received, shipped, whatever, but the manager hadn't been available. When I went back later, the place was already closed, so I sweet-talked my way past a very young security guard. He let me wander through the warehouse after hours to get a feel for the layout. I had planned to return the next day to talk to the manager." She shrugged. "As I told Detective Villanueva on the phone before you came home, my guess is the guard took off for the hills when the fire started."

"So all these memories you were having were your character's, not yours?"

"Not all of them, but most. Some were actually mine. The dream I had about my apartment, hearing that woman's voice and the boarding school, those were definitely real. The red hankie with the mono-grammed *V* is real, too. It was my mother's. Her name was Virginia."

Cale tried to absorb everything Maggie—Amanda—was telling him. As crazy as it all sounded, he couldn't help the huge surge of relief that he'd been right. She wasn't "Maggie LaRue." "I don't know which is more strange," he admitted. "The dreams you thought were legitimate or the fact that your characters are that real to you."

She laughed nervously. "Just wait until I start talking to myself."

There wasn't a single reason he should be shocked by her statement. Not after everything they'd gone through already. "Do you answer?"

She bit her bottom lip. "All the time," she replied sheepishly.

"I'm sure they have warehouses throughout New York. Why come all the way to California?"

"Because I'm setting the book here," she explained. "I like to take a few weeks and...*absorb*, I guess you could call it, an area. Before the accident, I spent a lot of time down on the docks in Long Beach, took in the atmosphere along Rodeo Drive and the Santa Monica Pier. Unfortunately, I spent a lot of money on Rodeo, so much that I'd even bought an extra suitcase."

He glanced over at the bags he hadn't even noticed until now, stacked neatly beside the desk. A sense of dread filled him at the reminder that she would be leaving in a matter of days. Unless he could convince her to stay.

"Where were they?" he asked with an inclination of his head toward the suitcases.

"In the bungalow I'd rented for the month. Tilly helped me pack and bring my things here. I hope you don't mind. It's going to take a few days for me to get my things in order before I go back to New York."

"Yes," he said suddenly. "I do mind. I mind a great deal."

Her mouth formed a perfect *O* as she stared at him in disbelief.

He shot off the sofa, needing to move, to quell the restlessness settling around his heart at the reminder that he had absolutely no ties to her. That she had no reason to remain in California another minute.

No, that wasn't right. She had no reason to remain with him, that's what he minded. But she did, and he planned to make her see it.

"I mind a whole hell of a lot that you're going back to New York," he said sharply.

"Cale—"

"Don't go," he said before she had the chance to issue a list of arguments to the contrary. "Stay here. Stay with me."

"But—"

"Look, I know you don't need me to take care of you, but dammit, you do need me, Maggie." She needed him to love her.

A sweet smile tugged her lips. "Amanda," she quietly corrected him.

He shoved his hand through his hair. "Maggie. Amanda. Hell, I don't care if your name is Persephone."

"Cale—"

"Is there someone else?" he interrupted her again. God, now that she'd recovered her memory, maybe there was some guy in her life. He hadn't even considered the possibility. No, he didn't buy it. There wasn't a snowball's chance of another man in her life. There couldn't be, not the way she'd loved him and gifted him with her heart and her body. Not a chance in hell.

"No," she said. "There's no one else."

He didn't think so, but it sure made him feel a whole lot better hearing her say it.

He circled the table and crouched in front of her, taking both of her hands in his. "Then what's stopping you from saying yes, you'll stay? Dammit, you need me...Amanda."

The name felt foreign to him. To him, she was Maggie.

Her eyes filled with a tenderness so touching, his heart ricocheted in his chest, then beat a heavy, slow rhythm.

"Three little words, Cale. Just three of them."

Her meaning registered. "Oh. Those."

"Hmm. Yes." A teasing light brightened her gaze. "Those."

"Don't you know, sweetheart? Don't you know I'd move heaven and earth for you?"

Her smiled softened. When she looked at him, he didn't doubt for a minute she loved him.

"Of course I know," she said gently. "A girl just likes to hear them."

The words she longed to hear lodged in his throat.

He could do this, he thought. He had to, since she wasn't giving him much choice in the matter. "You're not going to make this easy, are you?"

She answered by lacing the fingers of her good hand with his in a silent offer of encouragement.

"My dad loved my mom," he started slowly. "He loved her so much that when she died, he stopped living. He tried at first, but we knew he was faking it and after a while, he gave up completely.

"There's another reason I was late tonight," he continued. "A call came in that Brady and I took. It was one of our frequent flyers, a regular. She's dying of lung cancer and there isn't anything I can do to save her."

Compassion lined her features. "I'm so sorry."

"It wasn't that I *couldn't* help her," he explained. "We could've taken her to the E.R., and they might have been able to take whatever measures necessary to keep her alive. But she and her husband wouldn't *let* us. He said the greatest gift of love he could give his wife was to let her find peace.

"I don't want to end up like my old man did when my mom died, giving up the way he did. On himself and us kids."

She reached for him and traced her fingers lightly along his jaw. Determination and love shone in her eyes as she leveled her gaze on him. "You said I need you. Why, Cale? Why do I need you?" she asked, her voice barely above a whisper.

He swallowed, hard, and stared at her. He cleared his throat, not once, but twice. "You need me to love you...for the rest of your life."

Her smile wavered slightly. "And?"

He drew a deep cleansing breath into his lungs, not because he needed courage, but because he wanted to guarantee his next words were spoken loud and clear.

"I love you," he said confidently. "I love you, Amanda Hayes. Stay and let me show you just how much I do love you."

Her eyes filled with unshed tears, but the smile curving her luscious mouth chased away any lingering fear that might have remained in his heart. "Yes," she whispered.

"Yes? Yes, you'll stay?"

Her head bobbed up and down, then she wrapped her arms around his neck and plastered her body against his.

After a moment, she pulled back to look into his eyes. "I love you, Cale. And yes, I do need you to love me. In fact, I'm counting on it."

Love filled his heart and spread deep into his soul. He loved this woman with every ounce of heart, his body, his soul. This crazy, lovable, woman who'd come crashing into his life and turned it upside down with her own special brand of love. A love he didn't doubt for a second was healthy, and real. A love he'd never been able to imagine for himself...until now. Until Amanda.

# Epilogue

*Three months later*

AMANDA ADORED Sunday mornings when Cale was off duty. Who wouldn't be crazy about beginning the day with fresh croissants, plump red strawberries and gourmet coffee in bed, while sharing the Sunday paper with the man of her dreams? No Sunday morning would be complete if they didn't make love, either. A sexy, pleasurable bonus, in her opinion.

She put her half-empty mug on the bedside table, then readjusted the pillows behind her for the third time. She tested the padding, finally rid of the odd lump that had been pressing into her back.

"Amanda?"

"Hmm?" She rifled through the newspaper stacked between them for the entertainment section, since Cale had beat her to the crossword puzzle this morning.

"What's a four-letter word for determined?"

She looked at him, but his attention was on the puzzle. "*Grit,*" she offered. Since when did he need her help with a crossword? He usually leaned over her and spouted half the answers before she had a chance to fill in the squares herself.

"Nope. Ends with an *L.*"

She thought for a moment. *"Will?"*

He nodded absently, but she caught the hint of a grin teasing the curve of his mouth.

Relocating to California had been a lot less complicated than she'd imagined. Rather than selling her Manhattan loft, she'd decided to keep it as an investment and rent it out with the assistance of a property management company. Her father and stepmother hadn't been thrilled with her moving across the country, but she'd held her ground as she always did when something was important to her. Once her parents had met Cale and realized how incredibly happy he made her, they accepted her decision.

Bored with the Hollywood happenings, she tossed the entertainment news aside for the home and garden section. Decorating and gardening had become two of her new favorite pastimes recently. There was something incredibly seductive about having a man shoveling dirt beneath the warm sunshine. When he'd shed his T-shirt, she was powerless to keep her hands off all that rippling muscle and sweat-moistened skin. Even with her imagination, she never dreamed making love in a garage could be so erotic.

She let out a little contented sigh at the recent memory, then reached beneath the sheet with her foot and smoothed her toes along Cale's bare thigh. A much more interesting prospect than the latest in dry-brush techniques she'd been reading up on.

"You should know this one." He sounded bored, as if the muscle in his leg hadn't flinched from her touch. "James Bond flick. Blank *Only Live Twice.*"

"You." She shoved the newspapers onto the floor and scooted closer to Cale. "As in I want to do *you*," she added huskily. "Now."

Instead of tossing the puzzle aside to take her up on her offer, he surprised her by burying his nose even deeper in the paper. If it hadn't been for his sharp intake of breath when she pressed her lips to his abdomen, she would have thought he'd become immune to her.

"Now here's a hard one." His voice was strained and she smiled. Cale? Immune? Never.

Reaching beneath the sheet, she took him in her hand. "Yes," she whispered, then traced the outline of his navel with her tongue. "Very."

A groan erupted from deep in his chest. "Hitched? Is there a five-letter word for that?"

He sounded so pained, she looked up and frowned at him. "How about a six-letter word for sex?"

She tried to snag the paper from him, but he quickly moved it out of her reach. "Amanda, I'm serious."

She knew him well enough by now to understand he was determined about something. Well, she might cooperate, but no way would she play fair.

Rising to her knees, she straddled his hips so the moist lace of her panties was wedged tightly against his erection. He eased out a hiss of breath through gritted teeth when she rocked slowly against him. "So was I," she said with meaning. "Hitched, huh?"

He nodded.

She wiggled her bottom against his thighs and almost groaned herself when the lace rasped against her sensitized skin. "Any letters?"

"*M*," he managed hoarsely. "First letter."

"*Marry.*" She smoothed her hands along his rib cage to his back, leaning forward to intentionally brush her breasts against his chest. "Too easy," she told him. "How about a real challenge?"

He tossed the puzzle and his pen aside, then ran his hands down her back to cup her bottom and urge her closer. "If it was that easy, you would've figured it out by now."

Curious, she tipped her head back, and her breath caught at the tenderness in his eyes. "Figured what out?"

He placed a quick hard kiss on her lips. "Think about it."

That sexy smile of his distracted her. "What is there to think about?" she said after a moment. "You've been playing stupid about simple crossword clues any twelve-year-old would've known."

He chuckled and held her tighter. "And the answers were...?"

"Will. You." Her eyes widened and her pulse rate took off like a shot. "Marry."

He loosened his hold to lift the edge of her pillow, revealing a small, deep-blue velvet box tucked beneath. "I thought for sure you'd find it when you fluffed your pillows," he said, plucking the box from the mattress. "But when you didn't, I had to think fast."

Slowly, he opened the box. Nestled inside the velvet sat a princess-cut diamond flanked by a pair of triangular-shaped opals in a platinum setting. He slipped the ring from the box and lifted her left hand. "I love you, Amanda. Will you marry me?"

Her heart filled to overflowing. "Yes," she told him without an ounce of hesitation. "I will."

The ring fitted perfectly. Just as perfectly as she and Cale fitted into each other's lives, she realized. He captured her lips in a thorough, bone-melting kiss, leaving her with no doubt exactly where they were headed—straight to paradise.

\* \* \* \* \*

*Get ready for*
*RITA® Award-nominated author Jamie Denton*
*to turn up the heat*
*with the second story in the*
SOME LIKE IT HOT *miniseries...*
*HEATWAVE*
*On sale October 2003*

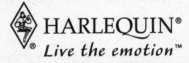

# Is your man too good to be true?

Hot, gorgeous AND romantic?
If so, he could be a Harlequin® Blaze™ series cover model!

Our grand-prize winners will receive a trip for two to New York City to
shoot the cover of a Blaze novel, and will stay at the luxurious Plaza Hotel.
Plus, they'll receive $500 U.S. spending money!
The runner-up winners will receive $200 U.S.
to spend on a romantic dinner for two.

## It's easy to enter!

In 100 words or less, tell us what makes your boyfriend or spouse a true romantic
and the perfect candidate for the cover of a Blaze novel, and include in your submission
two photos of this potential cover model.

All entries must include the written submission of the contest entrant, two photographs of the model
candidate and the Official Entry Form and Publicity Release forms completed in full and signed by
both the model candidate and the contest entrant. Harlequin, along with the experts at
Elite Model Management, will select a winner.

For photo and complete Contest details, please refer to the Official Rules on the next page. All entries
will become the property of Harlequin Enterprises Ltd. and are not returnable.

**Please visit** www.blazecovermodel.com **to download a copy of the Official Entry Form and
Publicity Release Form or send a request to one of the addresses below.**

Please mail your entry to: **Harlequin Blaze Cover Model Search**

| In U.S.A. | In Canada |
|---|---|
| P.O. Box 9069 | P.O. Box 637 |
| Buffalo, NY | Fort Erie, ON |
| 14269-9069 | L2A 5X3 |

No purchase necessary. Contest open to Canadian and U.S. residents who are 18 and over.
Void where prohibited. Contest closes September 30, 2003.

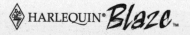

# HARLEQUIN BLAZE COVER MODEL SEARCH CONTEST 3569 OFFICIAL RULES
## NO PURCHASE NECESSARY TO ENTER

1. To enter, submit two (2) 4" x 6" photographs of a boyfriend or spouse (who must be 18 years of age or older) taken no later than three (3) months from the time of entry: a close-up, waist up, shirtless photograph; and a fully clothed, full-length photograph, then, tell us, in 100 words or fewer, why he should be a Harlequin Blaze cover model and how he is romantic. Your complete "entry" must include: (i) your essay, (ii) the Official Entry Form and Publicity Release Form printed below completed and signed by you (as "Entrant"), (iii) the photographs (with your hand-written name, address and phone number, and your model's name, address and phone number on the back of each photograph), and (iv) the Publicity Release Form and Photograph Representation Form printed below completed and signed by your model (as "Model"), and should be sent via first-class mail to either: Harlequin Blaze Cover Model Search Contest 3569, P.O. Box 9069, Buffalo, NY, 14269-9069, or Harlequin Blaze Cover Model Search Contest 3569, P.O. Box 637, Fort Erie, Ontario L2A 5X3. All submissions must be in English and be received no later than September 30, 2003. Limit: one entry per person, household or organization. **Purchase or acceptance of a product offer does not improve your chances of winning.** All entry requirements must be strictly adhered to for eligibility and to ensure fairness among entries.

2. Ten (10) Finalist submissions (photographs and essays) will be selected by a panel of judges consisting of members of the Harlequin editorial, marketing and public relations staff, as well as a representative from Elite Model Management (Toronto) Inc., based on the following criteria:

Aptness/Appropriateness of submitted photographs for a Harlequin Blaze cover—70%

Originality of Essay—20%

Sincerity of Essay—10%

In the event of a tie, duplicate finalists will be selected. The photographs submitted by finalists will be posted on the Harlequin website no later than November 15, 2003 (at www.blazecovermodel.com), and viewers may vote, in rank order, on their favorite(s) to assist in the panel of judges' final determination of the Grand Prize and Runner-up winning entries based on the above judging criteria. All decisions of the judges are final.

3. All entries become the property of Harlequin Enterprises Ltd. and none will be returned. Any entry may be used for future promotional purposes. Elite Model Management (Toronto) Inc. and/or its partners, subsidiaries and affiliates operating as "Elite Model Management" will have access to all entries including all personal information, and may contact any Entrant and/or Model in its sole discretion for their own business purposes. Harlequin and Elite Model Management (Toronto) Inc. are separate entities with no legal association or partnership whatsoever having no power to bind or obligate the other or create any expressed or implied obligation or responsibility on behalf of the other, such that Harlequin shall not be responsible in any way for any acts or omissions of Elite Model Management (Toronto) Inc. or its partners, subsidiaries and affiliates in connection with the Contest or otherwise and Elite Model Management shall not be responsible in any way for any acts or omissions of Harlequin or its partners, subsidiaries and affiliates in connection with the contest or otherwise.

4. All Entrants and Models must be residents of the U.S. or Canada, and have no prior criminal convictions. The contest is not open to any Model that is a professional model and/or actor in any capacity at the time of the entry. Contest void wherever prohibited by law; all applicable laws and regulations apply. Any litigation within the Province of Quebec regarding the conduct or organization of a publicity contest may be submitted to the Régie des alcools, des courses et des jeux for a ruling, and any litigation regarding the awarding of a prize may be submitted to the Régie only for the purpose of helping the parties reach a settlement. Employees and immediate family members of Harlequin Enterprises Ltd., D.L. Blair, Inc., Elite Model Management (Toronto) Inc. and their parents, affiliates, subsidiaries and all other agencies, entities and persons connected with the use, marketing or conduct of this Contest are not eligible to enter. Acceptance of any prize offered constitutes permission to use Entrants' and Models' names, essay submissions, photographs or other likenesses for the purposes of advertising, trade, publication and promotion on behalf of Harlequin Enterprises Ltd., its parent, affiliates, subsidiaries, assigns and other authorized entities involved in the judging and promotion of the contest without further compensation to any Entrant or Model, unless prohibited by law.

5. Finalists will be determined no later than October 30, 2003. Prize Winners will be determined no later than January 31, 2004. Grand Prize Winners (consisting of winning Entrant and Model) will be required to sign and return Affidavit of Eligibility/Release of Liability and Model Release forms within thirty (30) days of notification. Non-compliance with this requirement and within the specified time period will result in disqualification and an alternate will be selected. Any prize notification returned as undeliverable will result in the awarding of the prize to an alternate set of winners. All travelers (or parent/legal guardian of a minor) must execute the Affidavit of Eligibility/Release of Liability prior to ticketing and require passports required travel documents (e.g. valid photo ID) where applicable. Travel dates specified by Sponsor but no later than May 30, 2004.

6. Prizes: One (1) Grand Prize—the opportunity for the Model to appear on the cover of a paperback book from the Harlequin Blaze series, and a 3 day/2 night trip for two (Entrant and Model) to New York, NY for the photo shoot of Model which includes round-trip coach air transportation from the commercial airport nearest the winning Entrant's home to New York, NY, (or, in lieu of air transportation, $100 cash payable to Entrant and Model, if the winning Entrant's home is within 250 miles of New York, NY), hotel accommodations (double occupancy) at the Plaza Hotel and $500 cash spending money payable to Entrant and Model, (approximate prize value: $8,000), and one (1) Runner-up Prize of $200 cash payable to Entrant and Model for a romantic dinner for two (approximate prize value: $200). Prizes are valued in U.S. currency. Prizes consist of only those items listed as part of the prize. No substitution of prize(s) permitted by winners. All prizes are awarded jointly to the Entrant and Model of the winning entries, and are not severable - prizes and obligations may not be assigned or transferred. Any change to the Entrant and/or Model of the winning entries will result in disqualification and an alternate will be selected. Taxes on prize are the sole responsibility of winners. Any and all expenses and/or items not specifically described as part of the prize are the sole responsibility of winners. Harlequin Enterprises Ltd. and D.L. Blair, Inc., their parents, affiliates, and subsidiaries are not responsible for errors in printing of Contest entries and/or game pieces. No responsibility is assumed for lost, stolen, late, illegible, incomplete, inaccurate, non-delivered, postage due or misdirected mail or entries. In the event of printing or other errors which may result in unintended prize values or duplication of prizes, all affected game pieces or entries shall be null and void.

7. Winners will be notified by mail. For winners' list (available after March 31, 2004), send a self-addressed, stamped envelope to: Harlequin Blaze Cover Model Search Contest 3569 Winners, P.O. Box 4200, Blair, NE 68009-4200, or refer to the Harlequin website (at www.blazecovermodel.com).

Contest sponsored by Harlequin Enterprises Ltd., P.O. Box 9042, Buffalo, NY 14269-9042.

HBCVRMODEL2

**Your opinion is important to us!** Please take a few moments to share your thoughts with us about your experiences with Harlequin and Silhouette books. Your comments will be very useful in ensuring that we deliver books you love to read.
*Please take a few minutes to complete the questionnaire, then send it to us at the address below.*

Send your completed questionnaires to:
**Harlequin/Silhouette Reader Survey, P.O. Box 9046, Buffalo, NY 14269-9046**

1. As you may know, there are many different lines under the Harlequin and Silhouette brands. Each of the lines is listed below. Please check the box that most represents your reading habit for each line.

| Line | Currently read this line | Do not read this line | Not sure if I read this line |
|---|---|---|---|
| Harlequin American Romance | ❑ | ❑ | ❑ |
| Harlequin Duets | ❑ | ❑ | ❑ |
| Harlequin Romance | ❑ | ❑ | ❑ |
| Harlequin Historicals | ❑ | ❑ | ❑ |
| Harlequin Superromance | ❑ | ❑ | ❑ |
| Harlequin Intrigue | ❑ | ❑ | ❑ |
| Harlequin Presents | ❑ | ❑ | ❑ |
| Harlequin Temptation | ❑ | ❑ | ❑ |
| Harlequin Blaze | ❑ | ❑ | ❑ |
| Silhouette Special Edition | ❑ | ❑ | ❑ |
| Silhouette Romance | ❑ | ❑ | ❑ |
| Silhouette Intimate Moments | ❑ | ❑ | ❑ |
| Silhouette Desire | ❑ | ❑ | ❑ |

2. Which of the following best describes why you bought *this book?* One answer only, please.

| | | | |
|---|---|---|---|
| the picture on the cover | ❑ | the title | ❑ |
| the author | ❑ | the line is one I read often | ❑ |
| part of a miniseries | ❑ | saw an ad in another book | ❑ |
| saw an ad in a magazine/newsletter | ❑ | a friend told me about it | ❑ |
| I borrowed/was given this book | ❑ | other: _____ | ❑ |

3. Where did you buy *this book?* One answer only, please.

| | | | |
|---|---|---|---|
| at Barnes & Noble | ❑ | at a grocery store | ❑ |
| at Waldenbooks | ❑ | at a drugstore | ❑ |
| at Borders | ❑ | on eHarlequin.com Web site | ❑ |
| at another bookstore | ❑ | from another Web site | ❑ |
| at Wal-Mart | ❑ | Harlequin/Silhouette Reader Service/through the mail | ❑ |
| at Target | ❑ | | |
| at Kmart | ❑ | used books from anywhere | ❑ |
| at another department store or mass merchandiser | ❑ | I borrowed/was given this book | ❑ |

4. On average, how many Harlequin and Silhouette books do you buy at one time?

| | |
|---|---|
| I buy _____ books at one time | ❑ |
| I rarely buy a book | ❑ |

MRQ403HT-1A

5. How many times per month do you shop for any *Harlequin and/or Silhouette* books?
One answer only, please.

| | | | |
|---|---|---|---|
| 1 or more times a week | ❑ | a few times per year | ❑ |
| 1 to 3 times per month | ❑ | less often than once a year | ❑ |
| 1 to 2 times every 3 months | ❑ | never | ❑ |

6. When you think of your ideal heroine, which *one* statement describes her the best?
One answer only, please.

| | | | |
|---|---|---|---|
| She's a woman who is strong-willed | ❑ | She's a desirable woman | ❑ |
| She's a woman who is needed by others | ❑ | She's a powerful woman | ❑ |
| She's a woman who is taken care of | ❑ | She's a passionate woman | ❑ |
| She's an adventurous woman | ❑ | She's a sensitive woman | ❑ |

7. The following statements describe types or genres of books that you may be
interested in reading. Pick *up to 2 types* of books that you are most interested in.

| | |
|---|---|
| I like to read about truly romantic relationships | ❑ |
| I like to read stories that are sexy romances | ❑ |
| I like to read romantic comedies | ❑ |
| I like to read a romantic mystery/suspense | ❑ |
| I like to read about romantic adventures | ❑ |
| I like to read romance stories that involve family | ❑ |
| I like to read about a romance in times or places that I have never seen | ❑ |
| Other: _____ | ❑ |

*The following questions help us to group your answers with those readers who are
similar to you. Your answers will remain confidential.*

8. Please record your year of birth below.

19 _____

9. What is your marital status?

single ❑     married ❑     common-law ❑     widowed ❑
divorced/separated ❑

10. Do you have children 18 years of age or younger currently living at home?

yes ❑          no ❑

11. Which of the following best describes your employment status?

employed full-time or part-time ❑     homemaker ❑     student ❑
retired ❑     unemployed ❑

12. Do you have access to the Internet from either home or work?

yes ❑          no ❑

13. Have you ever visited eHarlequin.com?

yes ❑          no ❑

14. What state do you live in?

_____

15. Are you a member of Harlequin/Silhouette Reader Service?

yes ❑     Account #_____     no ❑     MRQ403HT-1B

If you enjoyed what you just read,
then we've got an offer you can't resist!

# Take 2 bestselling
# love stories FREE!
# Plus get a FREE surprise gift!

**Clip this page and mail it to Harlequin Reader Service®**

**IN U.S.A.**
3010 Walden Ave.
P.O. Box 1867
Buffalo, N.Y. 14240-1867

**IN CANADA**
P.O. Box 609
Fort Erie, Ontario
L2A 5X3

**YES!** Please send me 2 free Harlequin Temptation® novels and my free surprise gift. After receiving them, if I don't wish to receive anymore, I can return the shipping statement marked cancel. If I don't cancel, I will receive 4 brand-new novels each month, before they're available in stores. In the U.S.A., bill me at the bargain price of $3.57 plus 25¢ shipping and handling per book and applicable sales tax, if any*. In Canada, bill me at the bargain price of $4.24 plus 25¢ shipping and handling per book and applicable taxes**. That's the complete price and a savings of 10% off the cover prices—what a great deal! I understand that accepting the 2 free books and gift places me under no obligation ever to buy any books. I can always return a shipment and cancel at any time. Even if I never buy another book from Harlequin, the 2 free books and gift are mine to keep forever.

142 HDN DNT5
342 HDN DNT6

| | |
|---|---|
| Name | (PLEASE PRINT) |
| Address | Apt.# |
| City | State/Prov. | Zip/Postal Code |

\* Terms and prices subject to change without notice. Sales tax applicable in N.Y.
\*\* Canadian residents will be charged applicable provincial taxes and GST.
   All orders subject to approval. Offer limited to one per household and not valid to
   current Harlequin Temptation® subscribers.
   ® are registered trademarks of Harlequin Enterprises Limited.

TEMP02                                    ©1998 Harlequin Enterprises Limited

# COMING NEXT MONTH

### #945 ROOM…BUT NOT BORED! Dawn Atkins

Ariel Adams has to get her fledgling business off the ground. So she doesn't have the time—or the money—to fix up the beach house she just inherited. Tell *that* to the live-in handyman, Jake Renner. Despite how gorgeous he is—who knew that tool belts were so sexy?—she just can't let him continue living in her house. Too bad Jake shows no signs of leaving. Looks like she's got herself a boarder who will keep her anything but bored!

### #946 HEATWAVE Jamie Denton
*Some Like it Hot, Bk. 2*

Life for Emily Dugan can't get any worse. First, she loses her job, then her live-in boyfriend tells her he's in love with someone else *and* kicks her out of their apartment. Thankfully, she's now on vacation to visit her grandmother in California. When she finds out Grandy's cooking school has been plagued by a series of mysterious fires, Emily's shocked. But her surprise turns to instant heat when she meets sexy-as-sin arson investigator Drew Perry.

### #947 PURE INDULGENCE Janelle Denison
*Heat*

Kayla Thomas thought her dessert shop, Pure Indulgence, offered the ultimate in decadence…until she discovered some of her confections doubled as aphrodisiacs! Still, a little research wouldn't hurt…and restaurateur Jack Tremaine is just the test subject Kayla is craving. But will Jack's sweet tooth last beyond dessert…?

### #948 TRICK ME, TREAT ME Leslie Kelly
*The Wrong Bed*

After more than a year overseas doing research, true-crime writer Jared Winchester is finally home. Still, considering nobody knows he's back, he's surprised to get an invitation to an in-character Halloween party. His new persona—secret agent Miles Stone. Too bad he doesn't know that the party was actually *last* year. Or that gorgeous Gwen Compton will find secret agent men *irresistible….*